OUT OF ASHES

Phoenix Rising – Book 4

Alexandra Christian

www.BOROUGHSPUBLISHINGGROUP.com

OUT OF ASHES
Copyright © 2019 Rachel A. Wylie-Johnson

ISBN 978-1-948029- 61-2

To my sisters, Sarah and Jayel. I couldn't do it without you.

ACKNOWLEDGMENTS

Special thanks to all the Belles. When I wanted to give up, you guys were always there to encourage me. It means more than I can express in words. Also, there is no greater asset to a writer than a coven of fellow authors. I couldn't do any of this without the constant friendship and support of the Thursday Night Shenaniganators. You rock, ladies!

OUT OF ASHES

One

"Oh, sweet baby Jesus."

Phoebe sank to the edge of her bed, still clutching the tiny plastic tube between her fingertips. This had to be some kind of joke. Suddenly, she could hear her mother's voice in her head. *"You know what's wrong in this world? Everything's backwards. People are supposed to fall in love, get married, then have babies. That's how it's been for a thousand years before, so why change it now?"*

Phoe remembered the conversation clearly as being one of the last she'd ever had with her mother. They had been watching some sappy romantic movie in her hospital room. The flick was one of those estrogen-charged tearjerkers where girl meets boy in a bar, has a one-night stand, then shows up back in her hometown two years later with a toddler and a broken heart in need of mending. Phoe's mom had loved those movies. The only ones she liked better were the "Who the hell did I marry?" stories where the woman was married to her husband for three years before she realized he was a serial killer. Cautionary tales, she called them. A visual instruction manual about what *not* to do when choosing a mate.

And what had been number one on Marietta Addison's Commandments of Love?

"Never get knocked up out of wedlock," Phoe repeated the oft-told line aloud.

The tiny screen screamed her fate in large block letters: PREGNANT. How had this happened? They had been so careful. In fact, Phoe had changed birth control methods after their engagement to insure this kind of thing wouldn't happen. She and Cage agreed that while they were eager to be married, kids would have to wait. After all, their lives were too hectic and dangerous for a child. It was why their sort-of "adopted" kid, Ben—and, really, he adopted them as much as they had him—lived at school most of the time.

Then, there was Cage. There was no doubt in Phoe's mind that Macijah St. John was the love of her life. She had never been surer of anything than she was of his love for her, and that her decision to marry him had been the best one she'd ever made. But lately there had been some distance between them. She couldn't explain it, but she could sense it. Ever since they'd set their wedding date, Cage had been uneasy, restless, and grouchy.

These days, he snapped more often than he used to. They worked almost nonstop, and Phoe could tell that he was avoiding any talk of the wedding plans. Getting him here to St. Francisville for their engagement party had been a Herculean task. And now this. How could she possibly tell him?

"Phoe? Are you in there?" Her sister Jessica's voice was followed by a series of knocks that threatened to rip the door off the hinges.

"Yes. I'm here," Phoe called.

She sighed. She really didn't want to talk to her sister, or anyone else for that matter. She needed some time to process everything, and to do that, she needed solitude. Unfortunately, solitude was not an option today.

"Well open up the door," Jess groused. "Guests are starting to arrive and they're already crawling all over Cage."

Phoe couldn't help smiling. Of course, they were. This was the first time she'd actually invited people in St. Francisville into her life with Cage. And it was the reason why she had protested so vehemently when Jess suggested this party. People in this town were nosy gossips.

"I'll be down in a minute."

"Well can you open the door? I think I left my earrings in your bathroom."

"Why are your earrings in my bathroom?"

There was a long pause. "Because they're actually your earrings."

Phoe sighed and shoved the pregnancy test down in the pocket of her blue jeans. She had no interest in telling Jessica about the "delicate condition" quite yet. She would freak out and make a huge hairy deal about it. Then everyone at the party would know what was going on and Phoe would be completely humiliated.

"Do you even bother asking me if you can borrow my stuff anymore?" she asked, jerking the door open.

"You hate those earrings," Jessica said, pushing through the door. "Or any earrings. Or any sort of jewelry that makes you look like a girl." Jess wandered over to the dresser and fished the earrings out of the small box on top.

"Are you saying I'm not feminine?"

"No, I'm saying you aren't showy. And you really should be, sis. You're a beautiful woman, you know." She swept her hair back from the small hoop earrings, admiring them in the mirror.

"Thanks. I think."

Jess turned and started to reply, then suddenly noticed what Phoe had on and shook her head as if a tragedy had occurred. "That can't be what you're wearing."

Phoe looked down at herself. She thought her clothes were perfectly acceptable. Form-fitting jeans, a simple sleeveless white blouse with pearl buttons down the front, and a pair of leather flip-flops. "What's wrong with what I have on?"

"Nothing if you were going to dig up clams, but this is your engagement party."

"We told everyone it was going to be casual," Phoe protested. "I mean, there's a pig roasting in the backyard."

Jessica sighed. "Come on, sis. This is your in-person public engagement announcement. It's the most exciting thing that's happened in this turd town since the flood two summers ago when all the coffins in the cemetery floated down Main Street. Everyone in town is going to be here to ogle you and the sexy foreigner. You could at least make an attempt to look like the interplanetary woman of mystery we all know you to be."

"But that's just it." Phoe sighed. "I'm not an interplanetary woman of mystery. I'm Phoebe Addison, former librarian and two-time champion of the West Feliciana Parish Schools Spelling Bee."

"Don't be silly."

"You think I'm kidding? None of those people down there are here to see me. They can't believe that homely little Phoebe is finally getting married. They're here to nose around to try to uncover information that will expose Cage as some kind of British conman.

Or to see if maybe he's got some kind of deformity. It's like when Mom died. All those people who couldn't be bothered to come by and see her while she was sick, but they all showed up with a casserole in hand when she died."

"They wanted to pay their respects."

"Bullshit, Jess. They wanted to hear the gory details of her death. It's sickening. And this is the same thing, but less morbid."

Jess didn't catch the end of the rant. She was already in Phoe's closet, looking through the clothes like it was a job. Phoe had made a point not to pack too much on their trip from London, so there wasn't a lot to choose from.

"God, sis. That's a lot of beige." Jess stuck her head out of the closet, squinted her eyes and scrunched her nose. "Blech."

"Funny."

"You know, when I came to visit you and Cage in London a couple of months ago, you had great clothes. What the hell happened?"

"I didn't want to bring the whole flat. So, I brought some jeans and stuff. Most of the clothes in there are from before I moved."

"Back when you were a nun, apparently," Jess grumbled, pulling a shapeless, black sweater dress from the back of the closet.

"I don't know why you're being so judgey. You're an archaeologist. I've seen your closet. Most of your clothes consist of cargo shorts, t-shirts, and hiking boots."

"But I know how to dress up when the occasion calls for it. Oh," Jess cried out as she dug into the back of the closet and pulled out a sundress with big, pink polka dots with pink trim, and a lime green sash. "This is cute."

Had Jess taken leave of her senses? Phoe distinctly remembered her mother buying that dress, insisting Phoe wear it to some family occasion. She'd worn it one time for a total of three hours, then blocked that nightmare from her memory. "God, no. I still have a twitch from the last time I wore it."

"Oh, come on. It'll be precious on you." To illustrate her point, Jess came over and held the dress up to her sister. "Cage will love it."

"Cage doesn't notice my clothes unless I'm not wearing any."

Jess rolled her eyes and tossed the dress aside. "Well not wearing any isn't exactly an option on this particular occasion."

"Can't I wear what I have on?" Phoe whined, feeling like she was thirteen again.

Jess ignored her protests and turned back to the closet, rummaging for something acceptable. After several minutes, she emerged with another dress thrown over her arm. Phoe's breath caught in her throat. She recognized the dress immediately. It was the dress she'd been wearing the day she'd gotten the message from Jess that had changed Phoe's life forever. The dress was the color of a rainy day with large, brown mandalas screen-printed here and there. It was completely shapeless and fell to a little above her knee.

"What about this?"

Phoe took the dress from Jessica and looked it over. The dress gave her a chill. It was like looking into her past. It even smelled like the childish perfume she used to wear. She was certain she hadn't seen this dress since the day she'd left for the Canaveral Spaceport almost two years ago. She remembered taking it off and hanging it in the closet before opening the package with the medallion. It seemed like forever ago. She was a whole different person then, and the thought of putting on that dress made her feel as if she were putting on a costume of her old self.

"I doubt that old thing still fits," Phoe said. "I haven't worn it in ages." She crossed her arms over her belly. "Besides, it smells like moth balls."

Jessica sniffed the dress. "I don't smell anything. But if it will make you feel better, I'll go down and throw it in the dryer."

"Don't do that," Phoe snapped. "Please, Jess. Let me wear what I want to." She sank into the bed, turning away from her sister. All of a sudden, Phoe wanted nothing more than to talk to their mother. A wave of grief washed over her, and she could feel that familiar tightening in the corners of her jaw. Any second she was going to burst into tears and Jess was going to think Phoe had lost her mind.

She tried to choke back the tears, but it was too late. In spite of the fact that they'd never been particularly close, Jess knew her sister exceptionally well. She sat down beside Phoe and squeezed her hand. "What's the matter? There's about to be a lovely garden party down there in honor of your engagement to probably the most gorgeous man in the known universe. Practically the entire town is coming. All those bitches from high school that used to give you a hard time will be right there so you can rub your new, fabulous life in their faces. So why the hell do you look like someone who ran over a puppy?"

Knowing that she couldn't hide it any longer, Phoe reached into her pocket and pulled out the pregnancy test. She hesitated a moment before passing it over.

At first, Jess didn't seem to understand what she was looking at. She examined the test and Phoe could see comprehension dawning on her sister's face. "Oh my God," she cried out. "Oh my God, Phoe. This says pregnant."

"Good job," Phoe muttered. "I always knew you'd crack that reading thing."

"Ha-ha," Jess said, her tone completely devoid of mirth. She stared down at the test again, and then back to Phoe. "Wow. This… this is… wow. What is this?"

"I'm pregnant." Phoe hiccupped, then buried her face in her hands and began to sob.

"Oh no." Jess sighed. "Don't cry, Phoe." She threw an arm around her sister's shoulder and pulled her close. "This is a happy thing, right? I mean, you love Cage. He loves you. What's so terrible?"

Phoe sniffed and shook her head. "This wasn't supposed to happen yet. You have no idea how big a step it was for Cage to even ask me to marry him. He's already stressed about getting married; this could push him away for good." The truth was like poison, and suddenly, Phoe thought she was going to be sick.

Jess held Phoe gently, the way she had when they were kids after Phoe had fallen down and scraped her knee. "Come on. You know Cage won't leave you."

"No, I don't know that," she snapped. "He did not have a good experience with a wife and child before. And besides, what do I know about having a baby?"

"Probably more than most," Jess stated. She pushed Phoe's hair away from her brow and smiled. For the first time, she noticed how much Jess looked like their mother. "You've always been a caretaker, Phoe. You'll be a great mom."

Phoe shrugged. "Taking care of adults is different. What if I do something that makes the kid sick? And what about the Splice? I don't even know if I can carry a baby now that I'm… different."

Jess waved off Phoe's concerns. She was nothing if not optimistic. "Of course, you can. Everything is going to be fine. Stop worrying so much. That's always been your worst quality."

A knock at the door interrupted their little heart-to-heart. Phoe's belly rolled over at the thought of greeting any distant relations or well-meaning neighbors. She wasn't ready for this.

"Phoe, love. Are you in there?"

Cage. Of course, it was him. She'd left him downstairs in the kitchen with Miss Ava making paper-thin slices of lemon to float in the tea pitcher. Phoe loved the old woman, but she was almost certain that Miss Ava was giving Cage explicit instructions on holding the knife, slicing the lemons perfectly even, and placing them artfully in the pitcher.

"Yeah, I'm here," Phoe answered.then turned to Jess. "Not one word about this."

"Phoe, I really think you're worrying over nothing," Jess whispered.

"Not one word." Phoe went to the door and opened it to see Cage standing in the hall. He looked extremely uncomfortable and out of his element. His dark hair, which normally fell in haphazard waves over his brow, had been cut close and styled impeccably by the town stylist that morning. He'd traded his usual uniform of black pants and a close-fitting black shirt for khaki pants and a crisp blue shirt that made his eyes glow electric.

"What happened to you?" Phoe asked before she could stop herself.

"What do you mean?" he asked back.

She gestured at his clothes and hair, unable to make any noise that would describe him accurately. "This."

"I know. I look like someone's dad, come to pick them up from school."

She barked a nervous guffaw at his observation. "You look nice," she told him.

Cage looked from Phoe to Jess and back to Phoe. "Are you all right?"

"Of course, I am," she replied.

"She's nervous about the party," Jess shared helpfully. "You know how our Phoe is. She gets nervous and flustered around people." Jess gave Phoe's shoulder a squeeze and handed her the dress. "I think I'll let you finish changing. Y'all be good, now," she drawled with a parting wink and closed the door behind her.

"Do I really look that bad?" Cage asked, smoothing down his shirt. "That lady at the salon practically skinned my scalp. Then Ava showed up with these clothes. She thought I ought to look less… How did she put it? European."

Phoe chuckled and brushed her fingertips along his jawline before kissing his lips. "You look great. Everyone's going to love you."

"I hate things like this," he grumped. "I feel like I'm being paraded around like a prized Christmas goose."

"I know, and I'm sorry. It was a moment of weakness letting Jess and Miss Ava talk me into this. They played the 'it's what Mom would have done' card."

"Well I feel ridiculous," he grumbled. "Not to mention that I've been standing in the kitchen for fifteen minutes with this dreadful man who keeps looking through all the cupboards while humming 'God Save the King.'"

"Harold has always been odd. We ignore his little idiosyncrasies."

"And there's all this strange food everywhere. People keep bringing in covered plates filled with positively unidentifiable dishes of I don't know what. One lady brought some kind of green sludge with what looked disturbingly like bugs floating in it. There are at least three dishes with tiny sandwiches, one of which has this fluorescent orange paste on it."

Something about his reaction to congealed salad and pimento cheese struck Phoe as wildly funny, and she laughed until tears were running over her cheeks. He stared, completely oblivious to the joke until he was laughing too.

"Why are we laughing?"

"You were so… serious." She giggled. "It's like you've stepped onto another planet."

"Other planets aren't this weird," he humphed. He stared at the dress Jess had handed him. "Is this what you're wearing?"

"I guess." Phoe shrugged. "Jess thinks I need to wear something dressier today."

"I wouldn't take fashion advice from Jess."

"That was my thought."

"Good," he said, throwing the dress aside. "That dress isn't really you at all. It's much too bland. Too beige." He wrapped his arms around Phoe's waist and pulled her in for a soft kiss. She loved his kisses. When he took her lower lip between his and nibbled gently, a funny tingling began in her chest and worked its way down to hover over her sex. His large, calloused hands slid sneakily under her blouse and stroked at the hollow at the base of her spine. When he did that, she wanted to jump his bones.

And he knew it.

"Stop," she purred, pulling away from him.

"Why?"

"Because if you don't, we're going to miss our own party."

"I thought you didn't want to go anyway."

"But if we don't show up, Jess will come up here looking for us," Phoe purred, kissing his chin.

Cage growled and flashed his vampire eyes. "Bet she won't do it again."

"I'm not scared of seeing your naked ass, St. John," Jess called from the hall. Evidently, she'd been listening the whole time.

They gazed at one another then glanced toward the door. Phoe knew that Cage was weighing his options. The wrath of Miss Ava might be less frightening than the thought of the inevitable interrogations that would surely take place today.

"I guess we should go." Phoe gave in. She closed her eyes and took a deep breath. It was on the tip of her tongue to tell him about the baby. Maybe if she spit it out, it would be easier. At the last second, the words wouldn't come. "The sooner we get down there, the sooner it will be over, right?"

"One can only hope."

Two

The enormous farmhouse that Phoe called home was a breathtaking example of southern architecture. While there were no neoclassical columns or high widows' walks, the house looked like something straight out of a Faulkner novel.

Phoe and Cage stepped out onto the wide porch and winced at the screech of the screen door. The smell of barbeque wafted over the backyard like a heavenly fog. Miss Ava and Jessica had outdone themselves with this little soiree. Long tables swathed in white linen formed an L-shaped buffet of food. While most people had insisted on bringing something to share, Miss Ava had also hired a caterer with servers in little white jackets to take care of the big stuff, and a full bar was set up under one of the trees. The sun had started to set and Phoe noticed that someone had strung tiny lights in the trees and in crisscrossed strands across the yard that twinkled in the twilight.

"Phoe, Look at that cake." Ben crashed into Phoe, hugging her tightly in his excitement. "Miss Ava said I could have the first piece. Can I have the first piece?"

Phoe chuckled and ruffled Ben's hair. "Honestly, child, you act as if you've never had cake before." It wouldn't surprise her if he hadn't. The poor thing had spent most of his nine years on that desolate wasteland of a planet, Kobi Six.

"It's the biggest cake I ever saw."

"Ever seen," Cage corrected.

Ben wrinkled his nose and squeezed Phoe again. "Can I have the first piece?"

Phoe bent over and kissed the boy on top of the head. "You have whatever you like, dearest. Just save some for us."

"Hurray," Ben whooped, then scampered off toward the dessert table.

"That kid is a bottomless pit," Cage grumbled. "It's a good thing he goes away to school. We'd never have the money to feed him otherwise."

Phoe bit the inside of her mouth. Babies didn't eat that much. Perhaps Cage wouldn't notice the food bill for a while. Sighing, she took in the festivities. She was gobsmacked by the lengths to which her friends and family had gone to make this party. The decorations, the food, sending out invitations all over the galaxy—it was too much.

"Wow," Phoe said. "Y'all didn't have to go to all this trouble."

Jess giggled and wound her arm around Phoe's waist from the other side. "Of course we did, sis." Jess turned to Phoe, looking serious. "You're the only sister I have. I know we haven't always seen eye to eye, but you're my best friend. Not to mention saving my life and stuff."

Phoe smiled and hugged Jess tightly. "Ditto. I mean, if it hadn't been for you, none of this would be happening."

"You may not be thanking me for long," Jess said, nodding toward their Aunt Lena making her way toward them while trying to clutch a nasty little Chihuahua under one arm and an enormous purse in the other. Phoe was sure that purse already housed half the plated hors d'oeuvres weighing it down. Aunt Lena was actually their mother's aunt, and she was an insufferable biddy. Critical of everyone and everything that didn't line up with her own sheltered little view of the world, she was constantly telling them that they were wasting their lives by not getting married and having children as God had intended. Since she was certain she was right about everything, she was always in everyone's business.

"Phoebe. I'm so happy for you, dear. After all this time, I was beginning to think you'd be an old maid." She embraced Phoe, planting a juicy, hot pink kiss on her cheek. "Especially after... you know…"

Phoe could barely breathe in the old woman's bear hug. She knew exactly what the "you know" in question was, and she said a silent prayer that Lena wouldn't bring it up. The attack Phoe suffered in New Orleans a few years ago was not something she had shared with Cage, and now was not the appropriate time.

"I'm so glad you came, Aunt Lena," Jessica gushed falsely, rescuing Phoe from the crone's clutches. "Have you met the dashing Mr. St. John?"

Cage, hearing his name, immediately snapped to attention. "She most definitely has not," Cage said, emphasizing his posh-boy accent enough to make the poor woman blush and giggle in spite of herself. "I would have remembered such a beautiful lady." He took Aunt Lena's hand and kissed the back of it dramatically.

"Oh," she squealed, as if Cage might be the king of England himself. "The pleasure is mine."

Phoe's nausea returned.

"And what a cute puppy," Cage noted, reaching out to pat the tiny dog. It growled and snapped at him.

"Beau," Aunt Lena scolded. "That isn't polite."

"It's quite all right," Cage demurred. "Perhaps he's overly stimulated." That was a polite way of putting it. The dog's ill disposition was only surpassed by its ugliness.

"What the hell is wrong with that dog?" Cage whispered when Lena walked away.

"We're not sure," Jess replied. "She's had him for as long as I can remember."

"It's possible he's animatronic," Phoe deadpanned.

The three of them wandered through the crowd, playing the respectable hosts. Phoe could tell that Cage was uncomfortable. He held her hand so tightly that she was certain she heard the bones crack. People flitted around them in a garish parade of southern hospitality. Phoe had brought Cage back to St. Francisville several times over the course of their relationship, but she'd always been careful to keep her presence quiet. Mostly because she knew that this sort of situation was likely.

In the strange, futuristic world they lived in, St. Francisville was largely untouched. People still drove regular cars, cooked on electric stoves, did their shopping in the tiny market on Main Street, and observed the traditions of their parents and grandparents. If Cage, Phoe, or Jess let slip to any of these fine folks the existence of vampires, space colonies, or *aquilaton* cooking, they'd probably think one or all of them had lost their minds. Sure, they had televisions and eSlates. They watched the news like everyone else, but for some reason, the future hadn't caught up with St. Francisville

18

quite yet. Phoe thought she liked it better that way, but whenever she was home, she felt like Frodo at the end of *Lord of the Rings*. Innocence lost.

"How have I never met any of these people before?" Cage asked.

"By design, dearest."

"What do you mean?"

Jessica giggled. "She means that most of the people here are crazy. And I'm including our family members."

Cage shrugged. "Most everyone seems pretty nice."

Jessica and Phoe laughed together now. "Ah the great southern tradition of being 'nice,'" Phoe drolled. "If someone in the south is overly nice to you, it likely means they're plotting your demise."

"Bless your heart," the sisters said together.

"I don't think I get the joke." Cage shook his head.

Phoe threaded her arm through his as they walked along. "What we mean is, in a small, southern town, everyone seems nice. They ask about your family, who your people are, how you're enjoying your stay—lots of obligatory niceties, but what they're really doing is checking out the outsider."

"Exactly," Jess continued. "And when they're done, they'll all gather to evaluate your answers and determine if they were correct."

"There are right answers?"

"Oh yeah," Phoe and Jess responded in tandem.

"So, what if I give the wrong ones?" Cage asked.

"They'll make up stuff and look at you with disdain."

"But if you give the right ones," Jess said. "Then you're golden. You'll be combing old ladies out of your hair."

"But how do I know what the right answers are?" Cage asked. He looked even more terrified than he had before.

Phoe squeezed his arm and leaned in close. "See that man over there?" She indicated a short man in an impeccable seersucker suit with a bowtie, standing beside a little old woman who was so hunched over, she could almost touch her toes.

Cage nodded. "I spoke to him when he first arrived. He's a doctor or something, right? He seemed pretty nice."

"Doctor Mariette. He takes care of his Aunt Lorene, that ancient old lady beside him. Now, she's the meanest white lady in the county, but he's her lapdog. He'll do pretty much anything she asks because she's got more money than God. There's a school of thought that believes he's been slipping glass shards into her salads for the last five years in the hopes that one day, she'll shuffle off this mortal coil and leave him everything. She doesn't have any children and he's the sole heir."

"So, is he?"

"Is he what?"

"Grinding up glass into her food."

"Who knows." Jess shrugged. "But then there's that poor thing over there." She tilted her heat toward a wilted-looking woman sitting on her own under one of the live oaks. Her makeup was garish, and her hair had been teased up in an impossibly high pineapple shape. "Our mother's cousin, Flora. She used to live over in Calcasieu Parish, but she left the little town of Lake Charles in total disgrace when her husband Leonard was caught having an affair… with her favorite horse."

Cage's face was stoic, as if he couldn't believe what she was saying. "How—I mean…?"

"He claimed they were in love."

"Gracie Farquhar over there is nearly seventy years old, and supplements her retirement fund with a thriving cybersex holo-channel."

Jess kept going. "According to Miss Ava, Mr. and Mrs. Peacock standing over there by the dessert table have made numerous trips to the Gulf with Mr. and Mrs. Thompson."

"What's so strange about that?" Cage asked.

"By all reports, their relationship is quite close." Jess drew out the last couple of words while wiggling her eyebrows. "I had a friend who used to work for a lawyer here in St. Francisville. She said that almost every divorce in the parish began, 'So we all went to the Gulf for the weekend.'"

"The point is," Phoe explained, "small towns are weird. St. Francisville is downright bizarre. That little incident with Miss Ava's book club was a tiny tip of the iceberg."

Cage laughed, remembering Miss Ava's friends and their spiked teacakes. "I'm not sure that qualifies as bizarre. Little old ladies high on weed is probably more common than we think."

"Did someone say weed?"

Phoe turned to see her and Cage's friend Stefan Mueller strolling up to them. Jess tensed. Many bedroom conversations had been devoted to Jess's infatuation with Stefan and his boyish good looks. Blond hair, blue eyes, a solid build, and the slightest hint of a German accent were enough to make Jess positively weak in the knees.

"Stef," Phoe began, "I'm so glad you came." She embraced him and couldn't help stealing a mischievous smirk at her sister.

"Well, I couldn't let Ollie get on a plane by himself." He nodded to Oliver Manning, Cage's best friend, coming toward them, stumbling across the lawn. Phoe often wondered how Ollie and Cage ever became friends. The two men were opposites in almost every way. Cage was deliberate and precise in everything he did, from great feats of physical prowess to ordering his food at a restaurant. The same could not be said for the bookish Dr. Manning. Ollie had trouble walking across his own living room without falling.

For a time, everyone assumed that Jess would end up with Ollie, but after two dates, the pair had decided that they made much better friends than lovers.

"True," the sisters replied in unison.

"Who is this?" Stefan asked, glancing toward Jess.

"This is my sister, Jessica," Phoe answered. "Jess, meet Stef."

Jessica didn't look Stefan in the eye as he shook her outstretched hand gently. "We've met before," she mumbled.

"Have we?" Stefan asked. "I don't believe it. Surely, I would have remembered someone so beautiful."

Phoe had to stifle a giggle. For the first time in her memory, Jess was blushing. Usually, she was so poised and put together, but she shrank into a girlish mess at Stefan's charm. Hard to believe given Stef's colored reputation among the female population at the Bureau.

"It was only in passing," Jess said. "I'm not surprised. After all, you've got so many faces to remember."

"But none so lovely," Stef replied, holding her gaze.

Luckily, the awkward silence between the four of them was broken as Oliver crashed into Cage's back. "Oof. Sorry, mate." He held up his eSlate. "Looking at a message."

Phoe threw herself at Oliver, embracing him tightly. "I'm so glad you made it." She'd had a soft spot for Oliver since their first meeting. He'd saved Phoe and Cage's lives at Machine's mansion. She still felt a little guilty about what had gone down with Oliver's sister, Eve. He'd assured Phoe many times that he'd lost Eve years ago, and that he realized she'd had no choice, but Phoe still couldn't help wishing there had been an alternative. "We haven't seen you in ages."

"Are you kidding?" Ollie asked, shaking Cage's hand. "I wouldn't have missed this. We never thought Cage would get married again."

"He hasn't done it yet," Jess said. "Don't go putting the cart before the horse."

"Thinking I'll not go through with it then?" Cage teased.

"Not at all," Jess answered. "But I've known Phoe her whole life, and she can be pretty tough to take."

Cage kissed Phoe's forehead. "I think I can handle it."

Oliver didn't seem to be paying anyone attention, still poring over his eSlate until Cage punched his arm. "Oy, mate. What's so important?"

Ollie seemed startled that anyone had bothered speaking to him. He was every bit the socially awkward genius, and was often in his own little world. He looked up and blushed, clearly embarrassed that Cage had caught him. He closed the eSlate quickly and shoved it down into his back pocket. "Nothing. Sorry. I'd started to read this book on the plane. I guess I got too into it."

"That's our Ollie." Jess threw her arm around his neck. "Always got his head in the clouds."

"Not always," Oliver protested. "Sometimes I tune you out."

"Ouch." Cage laughed. "That's no way to speak to my future sister-in-law."

"She knows she talks too much. It's why our dating never worked."

"Maybe you never talked enough," Jess countered.

"Or maybe I could never get a word in edgewise."

Stefan wound a possessive arm around Jessica's waist and squeezed. "What you need, love, is a man of action."

Jess giggled and allowed him to lead her away into the crowd. Phoe watched them make their way across the yard. Jess threw her head back and laughed at something Stefan said, and Phoe couldn't help rolling her eyes. By the end of the night the two of them would be unbearable. Jess had a way of pretending to be aloof and bubbly, which usually drove men like Stefan crazy. The whole affair was unfolding in Phoe's mind like a holovid on high speed.

"I'm sure they'll be very happy," Oliver grumbled as if he'd read Phoe's mind.

"What do you mean?" Cage asked.

Oliver nodded over to where Jess and Stefan stood by the open bar. "Jess is a smart girl, but she's only interested in meatheads."

Phoe chuckled. "Oh, don't be so hard on Stef. He can't help it that he's beautiful."

Cage and Oliver groaned in unison. "I've known Stef for a while. He was a baby agent when I had my unfortunate run-in with MI Six. He's never been the sharpest knife in the drawer. And he's always been a man-whore."

"Are you saying that if brains were black powder, that Stef couldn't light a match?"

Oliver choked, doubling over with laughter at Phoe's summation. "As always, your country girl vernacular is a breath of fresh air."

***

Turned out that the party wasn't nearly as painful as Phoe imagined it would be. People were curious about Cage, but everyone was kind. Even her family managed to behave themselves, for the most part. Not that there were many among their number. Phoe and Jess were almost the last of their mother's family. A few distant cousins and Aunt Lena were it.

Their father had left when they were young, and he wasn't from St. Francisville. Phoe used to have this little fantasy that he would show up one day, begging forgiveness for abandoning them. At their mother's funeral, Phoe could have sworn she saw him standing at the edge of the cemetery, but it was most likely wishful thinking on her part. A tearful reunion hadn't happened yet, and Phoe didn't hold out much hope.

"You okay?" Cage asked.

Phoe offered a small smile and nodded. "I'm fine. Just thinking."

"Uh-oh."

"What uh-oh?"

"When you're sitting there quietly thinking, it probably means that you're worried about something."

"It does?"

Cage nodded. "Oh yeah." He leaned in and kissed her, gently sucking her lower lip between his. "You're also chewing on your lip."

Phoe laughed. "You know me so well. But really, I'm fine. I was thinking what a lovely party we're having."

"Indeed. Ava really outdid herself."

"I didn't think she'd be able to find this many people to invite," Phoe said. "In case you missed it, I've never been particularly good at making friends."

"Methinks you don't give yourself enough credit."

"Most of these people I haven't seen since high school. And I didn't particularly like them back then. Of course, there's also the family members I haven't seen since my mother's funeral. I was afraid that this was going to be more akin to a trip to the zoo, rather than an engagement party. But so far, everyone's been genuinely happy to see us."

"And why shouldn't they? You're a local girl made good. You escaped the small town and are having a successful life in the big city. Or so they assume, given your air of mystery." Cage straightened and puffed out his chest. "You're marrying a distinguished Englishman who works for the government. These people aren't being kind. They're in awe."

Phoe burst into laughter, startling the ladies standing near them. "Hardly. I think they're probably trying to figure out why the distinguished English gentleman is interested in a common librarian." Wisely, Phoe had not let anyone in on her secret identity with The Bureau for Espionage and Strategic Tactics. With the exception of Jess, her family thought she was the director of the Central London Archives. A glorified librarian. They knew that Cage worked for the government, but they weren't sure in what capacity. Phoe had observed much whispering, but everyone was politely curious.

"I hardly think 'awe' is the word for it," Phoe ribbed, but Cage wasn't listening. He was staring at something at the other side of the yard. She followed his gaze to where Maurice Wilder was stepping out of his car. Another man, who Phoe didn't recognize, was standing at the edge of the yard, talking to him.

"Oh wow. Maurice actually showed up. Is that his driver?"

"I don't know," Cage answered. "I didn't think he'd come, to be honest."

"Why not? He's our boss."

"Yeah, but I wouldn't call us friends. Not to mention that he's never been too jazzed about our relationship. Agents aren't supposed to have attachments, romantic or otherwise."

Phoe rolled her eyes. "That's ridiculous." She took Cage's hand and began pulling him toward the driveway.

"But probably wiser."

As they approached, they could hear Maurice talking to the unknown man who was turned away from them, so they couldn't see his face. His voice was low, as if he were trying to keep their conversation a secret. Maurice looked up, staring past the man to fix his gaze on Phoe and Cage.

Maurice was obviously nervous, shifting from one foot to the other. "We all made our choices. You would have done the same."

"Don't presume to tell me what I would have done," the man snapped. "And you're right. We did make choices. And this one is mine."

Phoe gasped as the man pulled an autopistol from inside his jacket and pointed it at Maurice. "Stop," she cried a moment before the man fired.

The noise of the autopistol rang out with a high-pitched squeal, frightening the flock of sparrows in the trees overhead. They flew off, and their wings created a fluttering din that blended with the guests' gasps. Everyone stopped, some looking toward Phoe because she'd screamed, others looking toward Maurice. He started to speak and reached out toward Cage who ran toward him. He fell as Cage reached him.

Then there was chaos.

Screams ripped through the silence and then everyone started running. They knocked over tables in their hurry, spilling food and champagne glasses everywhere. Aunt Lena clutched her nasty little dog tightly, running as fast as her tight-fitting pencil skirt would allow. Miss Ava, ever the level-headed one, kept trying to calm people as they blew past her toward their cars parked along the driveway.

Phoe looked around, searching the rushing crowd for Ben. "Ben," she screamed. Suddenly, the horror that he was hurt bubbled up from her belly and burned hot in the back of her throat. "Ben," she called again, turning around and scanning the scene before her and getting more frightened with each passing second.

"Phoebe," Ben cried, crashing into her side. He wasn't crying, but she could tell that he was close. His cheeks were red and his eyes full of panic. "What's happening?"

"Nothing," she lied. "Everything is okay. I want you to go inside the house and don't come out until we come to get you."

"But what about Mr. Wilder?"

Phoe's heart sank. She'd hoped that the child hadn't seen the shot. "He's going to be fine. Now do what I said."

He hesitated, squeezing her hand hard. For a second, she was afraid that he was going to refuse to go inside.

"Come on, kiddo." Jess jogged up behind them and put her arms around Ben.

"You've got him?" Phoe asked.

Jess nodded and Phoe took off across the yard. Cage still stood over Maurice, pressing a linen napkin against the wound that was slowly blossoming across his chest in an angry red stain. She started to ask what she could do, but then she caught a glimpse of movement in the trees beyond the house.

"Go," Cage ordered, pointing toward the woods. "I'll catch up."

She took off after the figure in black. At first, it seemed he didn't know she was coming for him, which gave her a chance to catch up. "Hey. Hey, you," she shouted after him. He only ran faster.

She looked down at her clothes dejectedly. "Could I not get through one event without ruining my clothes?" Then she had another thought. Would changing end her pregnancy? Would their baby be a shapeshifter? Hell, both parents changed into animals. Cage became a dragon for God's sake. The idea of what they may have created made her shudder. There was nothing for it. She had to be who she was, and time would tell if burning down to ash and rising again kept all the requisite molecules in place.

She closed her eyes and willed the burning to erupt beneath her skin. She'd learned to control the shift as much as possible, so it was quick. It still hurt like hell. Her scream of agony became the shrill squawking of the phoenix as she shot into the air. Her wings unfurled in orange, red, and yellow flames. She was careful to avoid setting the whole damn forest on fire as she swept down over the shooter's head. She circled him, thinking that perhaps she could trip him up. She squealed again, and the man cried out, holding his ears as he ran. He swatted at her, trying to avoid the sharp talons, but Phoe was able to dodge his attempts easily.

"Get away," he shouted, firing his autopistol in her general direction. Phoe felt the white-hot missile fly past her head. He fired again and grazed her wing. She pulled up fast, fighting against the wind resistance. In her haste, she didn't see the low-hanging branch waiting. She slammed into it, sending her into a tailspin. She screeched, watching as the man ran off while she tried to recover.

A loud roar sounded behind her and suddenly Cage was there. She caught a glimpse of him before the shift took over, leaving him standing on all fours as an enormous cougar. He roared again, and this time it sounded like a low gurgle and hiss. He stared down at her and she could see the recognition in his face. They exchanged a momentary glance and he took off through the woods after the gunman.

Phoe regrouped and shot off behind them in a streak of flames. Cage roared, and the man glanced behind. He stumbled over the underbrush, nearly falling, but managed to dive out of reach of the cougar's stride. There was another, tinny whine as the gunman fired his autopistol again. The plasma missile whizzed past Cage, singeing his fur and leaving a black streak. It only served to anger him further and he pushed faster through the overgrown branches. In the failing light, seeing through the inky atmosphere was becoming more of a problem. Phoe screeched, trying to guide Cage through the mist with the sound.

There was light in the distance and Phoe could hear the noise of traffic. The highway was beyond the tree line ahead. If the gunman made it through, they may never find him. She could hear the pounding of Cage's heart and the ragged breaths as he ran. He was tiring. The sun wasn't quite down, and Cage's vampire DNA always made him weaker in the daylight.

With a sudden leap, the gunman grabbed a low-hanging branch and swung away, barely escaping Cage's snapping jaws. With powerful arms, the assailant swung from one branch to another, keeping off the ground and out of Cage's reach. Phoe dove at him, trying to throw him down, but before she reached him, he broke through the trees and landed on the pavement.

A car whizzed by and the tailwind beat against Phoe's wings. Cage pulled up short beneath her and she lit at his shoulder. They watched as the car stopped and the gunman jerked the car door open and plunged inside. The tires screamed against the asphalt, leaving a long streak as it sped away.

Three

"Ollie has got to figure out how to keep a set of clothes with us," Phoe complained as the hospital doors closed behind them. Earlier, having to sneak buck naked past an ambulance, fire truck, three police cars and then make their way into the back door of her house was humiliating, and was starting to get old. Shifting and being visible while shifted was a much bigger problem on Earth. Particularly in a place like St. Francisville. Small towns in the southern US had not been as affected by Others as some of the larger cities. Most people down here still classified vampires and shapeshifters into the same category with UFOs and little green men. Letting the folks in St. Francisville see a blazing phoenix would likely incite a panic.

"Somehow, I don't think that's high on his list of priorities," Cage responded. His fingers flew across the screen of his eSlate as they followed corridor after corridor through the hospital looking for Maurice.

Our Lady of the Sacrament Hospital was not the sleek, futuristic medical center that was common in larger cities and the colonies. Phoe had been born in this hospital, and more importantly, her mother had died here. The sweet, sterile smell of antiseptic and cleaning supplies was enough to turn Phoe's stomach. The stark white floors gleamed under the harsh florescent lights, making her head ache.

"Are you sure you know where you're going?" Cage asked for the thousandth time. "Do you even know if we're in the right hospital?"

Phoe heaved an impatient sigh. Cage couldn't accept that in Louisiana they were in her territory. "Yes, Cage. This is the only hospital in twenty miles. It's the only place they would have brought him."

They finally arrived at a bank of elevators. Just as Phoe was punching the button, the doors opened, and Stefan was standing on the other side. "Thank God," he said, grabbing them both by their wrists and jerking them inside. "I've been trying to reach you for ages." He held up his eSlate as if to prove how inconvenienced he'd been.

"Sneaking naked through a crowd of people takes time." Cage gave Stefan a sidelong glare. "How's Maurice?"

"Still in surgery," Stefan replied. "The good news is, he hasn't stopped bitching the whole time."

"Oh good. So, he was conscious."

"It would take more than a bullet to take down Maurice Wilder," Stefan stated.

When they stepped off the elevator, the lobby was full of people. Ben ran to Cage and hugged him tightly. The boy's cheeks were flushed, and his eyes were puffy.

"All right, Ben?" Cage asked, ruffling the child's hair.

"I hope it's okay that I brought him?" Jess asked. "Stef and Ollie needed a ride."

"It's fine," Phoe replied. "We'll get him home soon."

"I wanted to ride in the ambulance, but Jess said I should stay with her," Ben explained. "Is Mr. Wilder going to be okay?"

"I'm sure he will," Cage answered. He led the boy over to a bank of chairs and handed him the eSlate. "Don't wander off, okay, kid?"

Ben nodded and curled up in one of the chairs. He began flipping through the screens of the slate, then looked up again. "That man isn't going to come back, is he?"

Phoe went to the boy and knelt down in front of his chair. "What are you talking about?" she asked, taking his hand.

"The man that shot Mr. Wilder," Ben said. "He isn't going to come back later, is he?"

"Of course, he isn't," Cage replied. "You don't have to worry, Ben. I won't let anything happen to you."

"You promise?"

"You don't have to be afraid, Ben," Phoe echoed Cage's sentiments. "Cage and I will always protect you."

The little boy nodded, but he didn't seem convinced. The events of the day had obviously left a scar. Phoe's heart broke for Ben. Wasn't this why they'd sent him to boarding school in the first place? Their lives were too violent and scattered to take care of a child. Phoe rubbed her belly absently.

"Fortunately for all of you, I'm never on vacation," Stefan said, beckoning Cage over. "I thought Phoe here might want some footage of the party, so I took the liberty of recording everything on my eSlate."

"That's really kind of you," Phoe uttered. "But I don't think I'll be creating any memory books from this day anytime soon."

Stef gave Phoe a look that seemed to express sorrow for her head injury. "True, but all scrapbooking aside, maybe we caught a picture of the gunman's face." He scanned through the images quickly. Evidently, Stef had walked all over the house looking through the different rooms. She could hear people talking, but the noise was muffled. An image of herself and Cage flashed by. They were standing on the back porch looking out over the party. Their fingers were entwined, and they looked so lovingly at one another as Stefan's camera zoomed in. Would they always be that happy? Would they always be that in love? Would Cage be able to love her when he finally knew all her secrets? She prayed he would. Looking at their image flickering on Stefan's eSlate made her heart ache with love for Cage. She didn't think she could bear it if he left her now.

"Phoe?"

"Huh?" She snapped out of her thoughts. "What did you say?"

"Anybody look familiar?" Cage asked. "After all, you probably saw more of him than I did. During a shift, I don't have much of an eye for detail."

"Oh… uhm… not so far," Phoe stammered. "Keep going." She watched the video flicker faster and faster. Then something caught her eye. "Stop. Go back a few frames."

Stefan stopped the video and began to click through still shots. Phoe took note of the timestamps. "This was ten minutes before the shooting started," she noted. "Keep going." Her eyes scanned the group shots. "I suspect he was there all night, slipped in with the crowd."

"Do you know all these people?" Stefan asked.

Phoe nodded. "Most of them. But of course, the whole damn town showed up because of Miss Ava. Some of these people I haven't seen since I was in high school, so I wouldn't know if they were strangers or not." Suddenly, she gasped. "Stop right there. That's him."

"Are you sure?"

"Yes. I recognize his suit." Phoe pointed at a man photographed at the edge of the crowd. He was all alone, smoking a cigarette at the edge of the road. "Can you get in closer on his face?"

"Sure." Stef zoomed in on the gunman. Almost as if he knew that he was being filmed, he stared straight at the camera—a middle-aged man, muscular, hair cropped close, wearing a pair of sunglasses that hid his eyes.

"Oh God," Cage said. "Stef, clear up his face."

"What?" Phoe asked. "Do you recognize him?"

"Maybe." He took the eSlate from Stef and enlarged the screenshot further. Slowly, the camera sharpened the image. "Damn. That's Damian Lasko."

"You know him?" Jess asked.

"He was a low-level tech geek." Cage nodded. "Retired from MI Six right after I started."

"Why would he have a beef with Maurice?" Stefan asked.

"I have no idea. I mean, he was basically a talented hacker."

"Maybe he and Maurice have history," Phoe speculated.

"Not likely," Stef said. "Cage can tell you. Maurice isn't exactly what you'd call a super-spy. More like an accountant. And Lasko was an IT guy who spent his whole career in basements staring at a computer screen. They wouldn't have even been in the same division."

"Before he shot Maurice, I could hear them arguing," Phoe told them. "The gunman said they'd all made their choices. Does that mean anything to you? I mean, I'm new here. You guys know Maurice better than I do."

Stefan and Cage shook their heads. "I don't think anyone really knows Maurice," Cage stated. "Besides, in this business, the less known about your colleagues is generally for the better." Cage started to say more, but the doctor came into the waiting room, clearing his throat.

"Doctor Ashe," Phoe called out, pushing Cage and Stefan aside. "Oh my gosh, I haven't seen you in ages." She embraced the young doctor, hardly able to believe it. "I thought you moved away."

"And miss all the hustle and bustle of St. Francisville?" Ashe replied, his voice tinged with sarcasm. "I was gone for a few years, but when my wife divorced me, I moved back here."

"Oh, I'm sorry to hear that."

"You two know each other?" Cage asked, inching closer to Phoe and winding an arm around her waist.

"Yeah," Phoe answered. "Jason and I went to high school together." Truth be told, Phoe had had a terribly embarrassing crush on Jason Ashe since grade school. They'd gone on one date senior year, but Jason had set his sights on greater things than St. Francisville. "He was our school's valedictorian."

"Hey, you almost beat me," Jason said with a slight flush.

"This is great that we all know each other." Stefan drew in an audible breath through his nose. "But could we get on with it? How is Maurice?"

Dr. Ashe regarded Stefan with a slightly annoyed expression, but then nodded and pulled an eSlate from his coat. "He's going to be fine," he replied. With a quick flick of his wrist, he scattered the image from his eSlate into a holographic image in the air before them. "The bullet passed straight through, barely managing to miss all of his major organs." He pointed out the wound on the hologram. "The good thing about autopistols is that the plasma missile, because of its temperature, immediately cauterizes the wound. So, he wasn't in danger of bleeding out. The real danger was the shock, which is more intense than with an old-school lead bullet."

"That's good, right?" Phoe asked.

Jason nodded.

"When can we see him?" Cage asked. "Maybe he can tell us why Damian Lasko tried to kill him."

"He's still unconscious, but he should come around in a few hours." Ashe gestured over his shoulder where a group of local police were gathered. "I think the gendarme are chomping at the bit to talk to him."

"They don't have jurisdiction," Stefan stated. "We'll take it from here."

"Begging your pardon," Ashe said. "The shooting did happen in St. Francisville, and I'm not going to be the one to tell the chief to get out. I'll leave that fight up to you, but I do have something you might find interesting." He flipped through the images on his eSlate until he came to a close-up shot of the bullet wound. It was a strange star shape, burned black around the edges with feverish red welts spreading out in a starburst pattern. "I've never seen an entry wound that looked like that."

Cage pulled the image closer and turned it this way and that, examining each layer. "It's new tech," he murmured to Stefan and Phoe. "So new I wasn't even sure it existed."

"What's so new about it?" Phoe asked.

"It's a slow-kill missile. The shot is actually the least of the problems." He looked up at Dr. Ashe. "Did you biopsy the wound?"

"We weren't going to, but those welts were a bit disconcerting. The surrounding tissue is completely necrotic."

"Oh no," Phoe cried out with a slight gasp.

"No worries," Dr. Ashe said. "We managed to stop the infection and your boss should make a full recovery."

"When can we see him?" Cage asked.

"As soon as he's conscious. But that probably won't be until the morning, so you all may as well go home and get some sleep." He leaned in and kissed Phoe on the cheek. "It was great seeing you, Phoe."

"You too," she murmured. She glanced sideways, and Cage's glare was practically murderous. "Thanks for your help, Jason."

The doctor nodded and was gone. While it was perfectly ridiculous that any man could possibly compare with Macijah St. John, it was still flattering to think that he might be jealous. It made her heart flutter and a slight heat settle in the pit of her belly. She weaved her fingertips through his and squeezed gently.

"Well, I guess that's it then," Stefan said. "There's not much more we can do tonight."

"Wrong," Jess countered. "You can take me out for some coffee. I'm too keyed up to sleep."

"Perfect." Stefan smiled, offering Jess a wink. Phoe wasn't sure that was such a good idea. While she loved Stefan for the sexy, empty-headed beast he was, Stef was a little too womanizing for her sister. Despite all of Jess's travels, she wasn't the best judge of men. "Don't the two of you want to join us?" he added.

Cage shook his head and gestured toward where Ben was nodding off in the chair across the room. "We have to get the kid home. He's dead on his feet."

"Suit yourselves." Jess shrugged. She jerked Stefan toward the elevator a little too eagerly. Phoe watched as they stepped inside, and Jess waved goodbye as the doors closed.

"I'm afraid that's a disaster waiting to happen," Phoe muttered.

"Oh good," Cage called over his shoulder while going to Ben and shaking him gently. "Exactly what we needed. One more disaster."

Four

The drive back to the house was silent and heavy. The day's events were preying on Cage's mind, but he wasn't finding any answers. Why in the world would Damian Lasko have a grudge against Maurice? And if he did, there were plenty of places that he could have gained access to him long before showing up in Louisiana at an engagement party. Why wait until they were in a small town on Earth?

Then there was the choice of weapon. Those slow-kill missiles were pretty rare. Only the most skilled of assassins with the Interplanetary Union would have access to such a weapon, and Damian Lasko was not an assassin. He was barely a spy with almost no field experience, at least to Cage's knowledge. But of course, secrets were their stock and trade, and Lasko could have worn that geek cover for a thousand reasons Cage would have never been privy to.

"You're awfully quiet." Phoe broke the silence with her soft voice. "What are you thinking about?"

"Maurice. The gunman." He looked over his shoulder to where Ben was asleep in the seat. "How I can't manage to have poor Ben in my custody for more than a few days without exposing him to violence and chaos."

"It wasn't your fault, you know. From what you told me, it's not as if violence was unknown to him before he met you." Cage barked out a hollow laugh. "I think he'll be okay." She tried to soothe him.

"This time. But what about the next?"

"What do you mean the next?"

Cage shrugged. "I don't know. Maybe I'm too tired and I'm not thinking straight." He paused, not sure how to word what he wanted to say. He knew that Phoe would take it as some kind of rejection.

All this talk of marriage had gotten him thinking about Corinne and Lily. There was a reason why agents weren't supposed to fall in love. Most cut all ties with family. It was the only way to keep them safe. Ever since he had asked Phoe to marry him in Absinthia, he'd been having nightmares about all the terrible things that might happen to her if his enemies found out.

"I know you pretty well at this point, St. John," Phoe poked. "You've got something big cooking in that big brain of yours, so out with it. What's wrong?"

"It's just that... I mean... do you ever worry about us having a family?"

"Do you mean, do I think about it?"

"Yeah. Do you ever wonder what it might be like?"

"All the time," Phoe admitted, and hated that she didn't have the guts to tell him the future was now. "You're the person I love. It's only natural that I want to have a family with you."

"Right. But do you ever worry that it might end badly if we did?"

"This is about Corinne," Phoe stated, her tone flat.

"No, this is about us," he contradicted. "Did you see Ben's face tonight? He saw Lasko pull out his autopistol and shoot Maurice. The boy was frightened. In that moment, he was that little boy on Kobi Six, abandoned and afraid."

"Of course it scared him. It scared all of us, but it's over now."

"But is it? Our life is a string of dangerous situations, one after the other."

"Yes, but it's not only that." Phoe turned to him in her seat. "You're right. You and I live a chaotic life, but it's also a wonderful life. You can't go back and change what happened to Corinne and Lily."

"I know, but—"

"You can't live your whole life being afraid. Don't you think she would want you to be happy?"

"Of course I do."

"And are you happy with me?"

Cage pulled into the driveway behind the farmhouse and threw the car into park before turning to face Phoe. He leaned in and took her face between his hands, pulling her close. He kissed her firmly on the lips, savoring her taste. That distinctly sweet flavor that never failed to make the blood rush hot in his veins. She sighed against him, opening her mouth and inviting his tongue inside.

"What do you think?" he asked. "How could I not be happy with you? You lifted the darkness and made me whole again. I couldn't be happier."

"Then don't worry so much."

"Darling, that's like telling water not to be wet."

Phoe smiled against his lips. "What I'm saying is, that no matter what happens, my life is better for being with you. And I cannot wait to be your wife."

She unclasped her seatbelt and drew closer. Cage pulled her into his arms, pressing her warm body against his. He needed to taste her. He needed to feel her writhing beneath him, to hear those tiny whimpers of pleasure. They'd been together for years now, but every time he kissed her, it was like the first time. He'd never thought he would ever feel this way about another woman. Phoebe Addison had given him hope, and the knowledge of that was more of an aphrodisiac than even the most intimate of touches.

"Are we home?"

Ben's sleepy voice quickly cleared the humid haze of arousal in an instant. Phoe smiled and flicked her tongue over Cage's chin with a playful wink. "Yes, darling. We're home."

They got out of the car and made their way to the back door. The only sign of their disastrous engagement party was a jagged strip of crime scene tape that still clung to one of the bushes.

"God, I hope Jess doesn't get too involved with Stefan tonight." Phoe stifled a yawn. "I'm going to need her help getting all this stuff back to the rental place." She motioned toward the tents, tables, and chairs that still sat lonely in the yard under the twinkle of the lights that had been woven into the trees.

"I'll help you." Ben yawned, which made her want to go to sleep immediately.

She ruffled his hair and squeezed him against her side. "I know I can count on you," she said. "But for now, how about going up to bed? You're practically unconscious." Ben started to protest, but his words turned into another epic yawn. He had no choice but to agree and tromped up the stairs to bed.

Cage opened the refrigerator and gazed inside. In the car, he'd realized how incredibly hungry he was. While in St. Francisville, finding blood was not an easy task, so he had to conserve his supply as much as possible. "A-ha," he said, pulling the narrow, stainless steel bottle from the back of the shelf. He opened it up and the lid made a hissing sound as the seal let go. Immediately, his mouth began to water, and his jaw felt tight. He turned up the bottle and drank deeply. The coppery flavor was a relief. He could already feel the warmth flooding his system. The exhaustion drained away almost instantly, and his eyelids fluttered with the overwhelming rush.

"Ava is such a gift," Phoe said.

Cage opened his eyes. "She is, but how so this time?"

Phoe gestured to the neatly packed containers stacked on the counters. "She packed up all the leftovers for us." She opened one of the containers and gasped. "Oooh...her famous tiny cupcakes." Phoe took one of the cupcakes and peeled the lacy wrapper off. "These are delicious. She used to make them for us when I was in her class." She hopped up on the counter and sank her teeth into the cake. "Mmm...you have to taste this."

Cage came over to where Phoe was perched on the countertop. Her legs were open, and he slid between them, placing his hands on either side of her thighs. "Are you going to give me a taste?" he asked, his voice a low purr.

Phoe offered a mischievous grin. Her tongue sneaked out to sweep away a tiny crumb stuck to the plump swell of her lip. "Do you want to taste my cupcake?"

"I can assure you, Miss Addison, nothing would please me more than to taste your cupcake." He leaned in for a kiss, but as he opened his mouth, she pressed the cupcake against his tongue. The fluffy white frosting was so sweet. He licked at it, almost sucking the cake into his mouth whole.

"It's good, isn't it?" Phoe whispered. She took another cupcake and offered it to him.

"Mmm," he replied. "We must remember to thank Ava for being so generous." He gathered the frosting onto his index finger and dabbed a bit of it on Phoe's lips. He leaned in and lapped at the sweet smear.

"More," she cooed, opening her mouth.

"Say please."

"Now." She grabbed his wrist and took his frosting-covered fingertip into her mouth. She swirled her tongue around it, lapping at the gooey confection. When she closed her lips around his finger and suckled gently, Cage could feel his cock spring to attention.

Without another word he swept her into his arms. Phoe wrapped her arms around his neck and allowed him to pull her off her feet. He supported her bottom with one large hand, helping her wrap her legs around him. One of the reasons he found her so sexy was that she made him feel powerful. Her body was compact and curvaceous, yet so small that she was dwarfed next to him. Her bosom was soft and plump pressed against his chest. It made his mouth water, and by the time they made it to the stairs, he was already tearing at her blouse.

"Take me upstairs and fuck this day away."

***

Phoe held on tight as Cage climbed the stairs. She could feel the strength in his arms where he held her. His step was light, trying not to let the floor creak and wake Ben. When he pushed open the door to the bedroom, Phoe was reminded of the person she used to be. This had been her childhood bedroom and it didn't seem right that she was bringing Cage here with such licentious intent. The bedspread was still the purple monstrosity that she'd insisted on at age fifteen. There were posters and pictures on the walls, and even an old teddy bear, but soon this room wouldn't be hers, it would be their child's.

Cage dropped her to the bed and climbed in after her. Phoe couldn't help smiling at his impatience as he tried to simultaneously take off his shirt and pants. "Be careful," she giggled as he nearly fell over the other side of the bed. "Don't hurt yourself." She got up on her knees and crawled toward him. "Here, let me help you out of Ava's clever disguise."

"Disguise?"

She brushed her fingertips along the strip of buttons on his shirt. "Yes, your 'respectable southern gentleman' costume."

"Don't think I'm respectable?" he asked, pulling off her blouse and throwing it aside.

"I certainly hope not." She pushed the shirt over his shoulders, baring his torso. Her heart gave a little flutter. "Even after all this time," she whispered.

"What?" he asked. His fingers played with the strap of her lacy bra, slowly moving it over the slope of her shoulder to kiss lightly.

"I love looking at you." She leaned in and lapped at the side of his neck. Her lips lingered over the pulsing, plump vein. Her hand slid along his collarbone and down his chest. The hard pectoral muscle jumped eagerly at her touch. "Touching you."

"So, you aren't sick of me?"

"Not at all. I'll never get tired of you."

"I find that so hard to believe. I'm pretty tough to live with."

Phoe smiled. "Not at all." Her hands drifted down to where the top button of his pants lay open and the zipper strained. Gently, her fingers drifted over the sensitive space below his bellybutton, tangling her fingertips in the soft curls and drifting lower. His cock was so hard that even the skin below it felt turgid. "How scandalous, Mr. St. John. If the sweet little ladies from the garden club only knew that beneath your sensible, pressed khakis was naught but skin."

"They're probably better off not knowing the truth."

Phoe waggled her eyebrows and shoved him back onto the bed. "Indeed." He laughed as she grabbed the waist of his pants and pulled them down his legs.

She caught a glimpse of herself in the mirror opposite. The deep navy-colored lace bra and panties clung to her form. They highlighted every curve. Her breasts practically spilled over the tight cups. The panties were cut so high that it was almost pointless wearing them. *How far you've come, Miss Addison.* Two years ago, she'd never have worn something so provocative, not to mention let someone see her in it. And now here she was, climbing astride this beast of a man and expressing her dominance. Mousey little Phoebe.

"What are you thinking about, love?" Cage asked, running his hands over her thighs.

"How much I love you," she whispered. She leaned over, kissing his lips. He arched into it, but Phoe pulled away, kissing down his chin and along the base of his throat. She could still smell the traces of his cologne and a hint of sweat from their run through the forest. The animal musk of the cougar still lingered, and it made her so wet for him, she lowered her silken-clad sex to the base of his erection. The length of his cock seemed to twitch at the contact, almost as if it were stretching and searching for some place to burrow deep inside. It rested against that sensitive valley below her opening.

"God, Phoe," he growled.

She smiled and undulated her hips slowly. "Not quite. But close." The delicious friction of his skin against the taut silk and lace felt so good. If she kept on, she knew that she would fall over the edge of her desire.

"You tease."

"Aww, I promise I'll make it up to you." She licked her lips and slid down his body until her face hovered over his cock. He purred as she breathed over him, her lips barely grazing his skin. He pushed his hips higher, but she wasn't having it and pulled away. He responded with a desperate groan. She crouched on all fours, hovering over him, and delighted in watching his body respond wherever she kissed or licked. She lapped at the thick vein along his length. Cage's breath was ragged, but he kept still. Every so often, she'd pull back and blow gently at the moist flesh.

"You're killing me, woman," Cage groaned, tangling his fingers in her hair.

"Poor baby," she muttered, then used the tip of her tongue to trace around the tip of his cock. This time he gasped, and his entire body tensed. This was where she wanted him: poised on the edge. It was his favorite game to play with her, but this time the tables were turned. One more touch was all it would take.

Finally, she backed away and knelt up. Her eyelids felt heavy. She was drunk with lust and she could feel his patience beginning to splinter. Reaching back, she popped the clasp on her bra, letting her breasts spill forth. Cage grinned, his eyes sparkling with need. He beckoned her forward with a finger. She nodded slowly and obeyed, crawling over his body and into his waiting arms.

"You're still a bit overdressed," he said, working his hand under the back of her panties and gripping her ass.

"Think so?"

"Mmmhmm…" He tangled the fabric in his hand and tugged. "I could always rip them off of you."

"These were expensive. Don't you dare." She leaned in to kiss him and he gripped her waist, throwing her down on the bed.

"Then I suppose I'll have to be gentle."

"Not too much, I hope." She grinned, batting her eyelashes.

His response was to roll her over, pulling up on her hips so that her back was arched like a cat in heat. "Hmm… This is a position I've never seen you in before."

"Yeah?"

"I think I like it." He pulled the wisp of fabric over the curve of her ass then kissed each globe. It was almost an act of reverence, and Phoe sighed. She felt his fangs, razor sharp and warm against the cool flesh. He nicked the skin gently and she could feel the tingle of his venom. "You're such an appetizing meal."

"One of these days you're going to eat me," she breathed, then gasped at feeling the sudden heat of his breath on her sex.

"The thought had crossed my mind." He bit down on the fleshy, outer labia, and she shrieked with surprise, but not with pain. Never with pain. His teeth grazed the tender skin and the venom created a sensation more pleasurable than anything she'd ever felt.

"Fuck…" Phoe moaned. "What are you doing to me?"

His response was his tongue plunging into her deep. The muscular organ was so insistent, working its way into places that had so far been untouched. Phoe groaned and pushed back, wanting more of him. He bit her again and this time she felt the blood begin to flow, mixing with her essence. He lapped it up, making hungry sounds—a man wandering through the desert who had finally found the ocean.

When he entered her, the stroke was hard and deliberate. Phoe's heart pounded in her chest in time with his furious thrusts. She could feel him deep inside, but it was more than that. His venom lay there, pooled on her skin, making her more sensitive. She cried out once more and knew that she couldn't stand it much longer. Cage hooked his arms around hers and pulled her back, crushing her body against his chest. He gripped her breast, squeezing the nipple between his fingertips until she screamed. He bit down on her shoulder as she came, and she could feel her life force flowing into him as her body climaxed over and over again.

Five

When Phoe's arm slapped him across the face for the third time, Cage figured it was no use trying to sleep. He rolled over and passed his hand over the screen of his eSlate. The projection clock glowed 3:28 overhead. He tapped the eSlate again and sat up. Glancing beside him, Phoe was fast asleep, mouth open and snoring softly into the pillow. He grinned and brushed her hair away from her brow. She still didn't stir.

He got up and pulled on a pair of lounge pants that were lying on the floor of the closet. Maybe a nice, cool glass of synthetic blood and one of Miss Ava's cupcakes would be the sedative he needed. Doubtful. The vampire DNA that lived in his cells was screaming that he needed to be awake and hunting at this hour. That was the only problem with taking up with humans. They tended to need sleep at night. His sleep schedule had been screwy ever since he and Phoe got together. The synthetic blood kept him strong in the daylight, thanks to Oliver, but his body still rejected the notion of sleeping at night.

The old, wooden stairs were creaky, and Cage winced with every step. He was trying to avoid waking up the entire house, if at all possible. He made his way into the kitchen and went into the fridge. Wedged in the back were a couple of stainless steel bottles of the synthetic blood that Oliver had formulated to keep him alive. Cage pulled one out and poured some into a big coffee mug. He looked down at the gloopy red substance with disdain. You could live on this shit for eternity, but why would you want to? It was kind of like the difference between a steak and potted meat.

He turned to put the mug into Phoe's ancient microwave when he heard the stairs creak behind. When he whipped around, Ben was there, yawning and still partially asleep.

"What are you doing up?"

"I had a bad dream," Ben mumbled, rubbing his eyes. "I was still on Kobi Six and we were being chased by these giant sand worm things."

"Did they have sand worms on Kobi Six?"

"I don't think so." Ben climbed up on one of the stools and stared at Cage. "What are you doing up?"

"I was hungry." The microwave dinged, and Cage pulled out the mug. He didn't really want to drink it in front of Ben. He had told the child precious little about this part of his condition and worried that the kid would be afraid of him if he knew the truth.

"But you have something to drink," Ben said, gesturing at the cup.

"It's uh—well—it's soup."

"Can I have some?"

"No," Cage answered, a bit more curtly than he had intended. "I mean, it isn't good for you to have something to eat so late."

"But you're eating."

"Yes, but I'm a grownup."

Ben sighed. "You guys always say stuff like that. I can't swear because I'm a kid, but it's okay for you. I can't have wine because I'm a kid, and it isn't good for me, but you guys drink that stuff all the time."

"You aren't missing much."

Ben was silent for a while, watching as Cage piddled around the kitchen and tried to avoid drinking his "soup." Finally, he asked. "Is Mr. Wilder going to be okay?"

"He will be."

"Are you telling me the truth?"

"Why wouldn't I be?"

Ben shrugged. "Grownups lie to kids a lot. At least Roman and some of the others did when we were on Kobi Six. Especially if something bad was going to happen."

Cage chuckled and opened up Miss Ava's cupcakes. He offered one to Ben. "I promise that everything is fine. I wouldn't lie to you."

"This kid at my school says that you're a secret agent and that it's your job to lie to people." He gave Cage a suspicious look and took one of the cupcakes.

Cage laughed and shook his head. "I wouldn't exactly call myself a secret agent. And yes, sometimes I have to lie to people, but never to you. Or Phoe." He took a sip of the synthetic blood. The back of his throat clenched with the bitter flavor and he gulped quickly. "Don't tell Phoe I let you eat that at this time of night."

Ben nodded, his mouth already full of pink frosting.

Cage was about to pontificate on the importance of brushing one's teeth after eating pure sugar when his eSlate buzzed angrily on the counter. He wondered who on earth might be calling at this hour. He glanced down at the screen and saw Stefan's name flashing in bright white letters. "God, what now," he grumbled before walking out of the kitchen, slate in one hand, mug in the other before picking it up.

"St. John? Is that you?"

"Who else would it be? Do you have any idea what time it is?"

"I know. Sorry, man."

"Is Maurice all right?"

"Yep. He's starting to come around. But that's not why I'm calling. I got a call from the NOLA police. They found Lasko."

"Dead or alive?"

"They didn't say. They told me they needed us to get down there as soon as we could."

"Address?"

"Coming right up, my friend." Cage heard the cheerful chirp of his eSlate as the location was sent to the device's mapping system. "See you in about an hour then?"

"Yeah. And Stefan? Don't go in without me." Cage tapped his eSlate and downed the rest of the synthetic blood.

"Who was that?" Ben asked as Cage walked back into the kitchen. He had a concerned expression that was somewhat marred by the mustache of pink frosting.

"Work."

"This late?" The boy looked doubtful.

"I know, right? Weird." He nudged Ben off his stool and gestured toward the stairs. "Come on. You have to get back to bed and I have to get going."

Suddenly, the boy had wide eyes full of terror. His chin trembled a little and he grabbed Cage's hand. "You—you aren't going to leave us, are you?"

"I've got something to attend to in the city. I'll be back before you wake up." He started steering the boy up the stairs and down the hall to his bedroom.

"But what if... what if..." Ben was on the edge of tears and his breath was coming in heavy gasps. "What if that man comes back?"

Cage stopped in his tracks. For a moment, Ben wasn't Ben. Maybe it was a trick of the shadows, but he could have sworn that the child in front of him was Lily. He left Lily behind for a job all those years ago, and when he came back... Cage knew that he wouldn't survive that again. His eSlate buzzed again in his hand as if to scold him for not coming faster.

"Cage?"

Cage knelt in front of Ben and brushed the tendrils of hair, still sweaty from sleep, away from his forehead. "You listen to me. Nobody is coming back here to hurt you. Phoe and I will always keep you safe."

"Are you sure?"

"I'm absolutely sure."

Cage hugged Ben tightly. His scars from Lily and Corinne still seemed so fresh. After their deaths, he'd thought he would never recover. But he did. Phoe had given him hope that there was still good in the world and that evil could still be defeated. "Now go to bed. Tell Phoe where I went."

Ben nodded and yawned. He was nearly asleep again. "Be careful, k?"

"As much as I can be. I'll be back soon." Cage ruffled Ben's hair and shooed him into his bedroom as his eSlate began to rattle impatiently.

***

The address Stefan sent Cage was questionable to say the least. In the two years he'd known Phoe, they'd been to New Orleans lots of times, but he'd never seen this part of the city before. It was like the city block that time forgot. Dilapidated row houses, abandoned warehouses, and sleazy motels lined the street. A small crowd had gathered around one of the motels where police officers worked to set up barriers and crime-scene tape. The sign over the doors said Hotel Gagnon. Cage parked the old truck that had once belonged to

Phoe's mother. He walked back to where the police cars were trying to block the alleyway.

"You're finally here." Stefan and Jessica jogged toward him. What were they still doing together?

"Where's Phoe?" Jess asked.

"At the house with Ben. What's going on?"

Stefan took a deep breath and nodded toward the rundown motel behind him. "We found Damian Lasko. Well, a homeless guy found him and flagged down a police officer. He's dead."

"Great." Cage wanted to curse that the asshole he wanted to question was dead, but more than anything, he wanted to get in the truck and head back to Phoe and Ben. "Please tell me there's a good reason why you called me out of bed for the death of an attempted murderer."

"Oh, it gets better," Jess said. "Come on."

The three of them started toward the motel. The place was crowded with rubberneckers and cops standing around. One of the cops made to stop them as they stepped over the barrier, but Cage and Stefan flashed their IU badges. For a second, Cage was afraid that they were going make Jess stay outside, but evidently that old adage about looking like you knew where you were going was true. No one questioned her.

As soon as they stepped through the ramshackle revolving door and into the lobby, Cage could smell the body. His vampiric senses were not always a blessing, he thought as he tried to breathe through his mouth. The stench of stale, diseased blood, piss, and mold permeated everything. A wino, presumably the one who had found the body, sat on an old couch in the lobby. He didn't seem to be disturbed in the least by a rat that gnawed at the cushion on the other side.

"I already told you, man. I came in here to get away from some dudes that was tryin' to rob me." The wino was feeling around in his pockets. His movements were erratic, and Cage could tell that any second, he was going to lose it completely.

Cage pulled a cigarette out of his pocket and gave the uniform cop a slight nudge. "Hey, mate," he called. "You look like you could use a cigarette." He held the cigarette out to him. The guy looked a little suspicious, but he took it and allowed Cage to light the end.

"Thanks, man," he said, taking a long draw and blowing it out. Cage's eyes watered with the smell of cheap wine and vomit-scented cigarette smoke. "These cops are hasslin' me."

"No worries. Relax, mate. I'm Cage." He nodded toward Jess and Stefan. "These are my partners. Can I ask you a couple of questions about what you found?"

"Man, I don't know shit. These two cats were roughin' me up for some cash out there at the corner of the alley. I ran down here to get away." He took another draw of the cigarette. His hands were shaking, but Cage couldn't be sure if it was from booze or fear.

"Did you see anyone in here when you came in?"

"The place was empty. Which is kind of strange."

"Why is that?" Stefan asked.

"You kiddin', right? The Hotel Gagnon is where you go to get whatever you want."

"So, it's a crank shop," Jess stated. "A flophouse slash whorehouse slash apothecary."

"But you were only coming in to get away from muggers," Stefan said sarcastically.

Cage sighed. "I don't care why you were here, mate. Just tell us what happened."

The guy nodded and finished off his cigarette. Cage had another waiting for him. "I went upstairs to sleep off this bad headache. There's lots of old beds still up there. I went into the first one on the hall and I noticed that there was somebody already lying there. So I was going to go on down to the next room, but then… I smelled… And there was flies all over the place…" He shook his head and dragged off the cigarette. "Man, I ain't never seen nothin' like that." He went into his pocket and handed Cage a wallet. "I found this on the floor by the bed."

Cage flipped open the wallet and saw Damian Lasko's IU clearance badge. Otherwise the wallet was empty.

He stood up and brushed off his hands where the guy had touched him. He handed the wallet over to Stefan. "Stef, stay down here with Jess." He handed the guy a couple of bills from his pocket. "Go eat something, mate."

"Cage, he's only going to put it up his nose or in a vein," Stefan started.

But Cage ignored him and started up a pitch-black stairwell. Cage wondered how the homeless guy ever made it up here in the first place without tripping and falling down. Cage closed his eyes and let the vampire take over enough so he could see. When he opened his eyes, everything was clear in shocking relief. Vampiric night vision was a bit like watching an extremely high-definition CCTV screen. Everything glowed in shades of blue and gray as it picked up the heat signatures to create a picture.

Looking down at the floor, he could see puddles of bright blue: blood. Cold blood, but blood nonetheless. He followed the splattered path down the corridor and into one of the old guest rooms. His gag reflex kicked in and he turned away, holding a hand over his mouth and nose to keep from vomiting. The stench was incredible. This wasn't the smell of something dead. It was something that had been dead for quite some time. But there was another layer beneath. An eldritch stink of some kind of dark magic. Cage had only smelled it one other time. Something truly evil. Something born, not some science experiment.

Cage forced himself to enter the room. Maybe it was his imagination, but the place was freezing. It was probably a blessing. If it had been hot, he didn't think he'd be able to stand the heightened stench.

The room was empty, save for an old lumpy mattress on a sagging bedframe in the corner. He could hear rats scurrying along the baseboards and inside the walls. The noise of city traffic was a constant din coming from the open window. With his vampiric vision, he could see the shape of something lying on the bed. It had an irregular shape, not like a body, but more like a pile of rags.

As he approached, the light from the police cars below brought things into focus. He almost laughed at his own ridiculousness. There was nothing there but a bunch of old clothes. But that smell, that horrible scent of death emanated. Then he saw it. Something wrinkled and black lay in the middle of the mattress. It had a moist, oily look. It seemed to be tangled up in tattered clothing. Cage pulled at some of the fabric and a black shirt came loose. He recognized it as the one Lasko had been wearing when he shot Maurice.

Cage threw the shirt aside, revealing a bloody mess. He assumed it was blood, but what it really looked like was black sludge. A hollow, limp skin lay amongst the bloody clothes like an animal pelt.

It had been split in several places like someone had been wearing the skin and simply unzipped it and left it lying here. Cage lifted it up, examining what was left of the face. The weight of it made his stomach roll over and he dropped the pelt to the floor. It hit with a wet plop.

"Jesus," Cage groaned, stumbling backward. "What the hell could have done something like that?"

Cage's commlink buzzed in his ear. "St. John. You okay up there?"

He touched the control piece on his hand. "I'm fine, Stef. It's Lasko all right."

"Think it was one of our guys caught up with him?"

"No. I don't. We need to get the body to Ollie as quickly and quietly as possible."

"What about the local police? They're not going to be too jazzed about giving up this case."

"They're going to have to deal." Cage glanced over his shoulder at the body again and shuddered. "I think this case is way out of their league."

Six

"You had no business going in there, St. John. BEAST is not to interfere in the affairs of local agencies. That is not within our purview."

"How can you say that, Maurice?" Cage stared out the window of Wilder's office, looking down on the city below. It had been a little over a week since the attack and Maurice was already back at work and bitching at him. Some things never changed, he supposed. "You and I both know that the threat on your life is anything but a drive-by shooting in a derelict city. We were in the middle of nowhere for fuck's sake."

"There's no reason to believe it's some big international conspiracy either." Maurice emphasized his point by banging a fist on the desk and then wincing in pain.

"Are you all right?"

"I'm perfectly fine." His tone was tense, and Cage knew Wilder was anything but finc. Two days after being shot, Wilder had insisted on getting on a plane and going home. Three days after that, he was back at B.E.A.S.T. HQ trying desperately to downplay the fact that he'd been nearly killed. "I don't know what everyone is making such a fuss about. My life's been in danger since the moment I stepped into MI Six."

"Yes, but few people have walked up to you out of the blue and shot you point blank in the stomach. And even fewer were former co-workers."

Wilder sighed and stood up. He went to the wet bar and poured himself a glass of bourbon on the rocks, making a point not to offer any to Cage. "I already told you. Lasko wasn't exactly a co-worker. He was a hacker that I'd met maybe once or twice." Maurice turned away from Cage and knocked back the tumbler before refilling it. He began to pace, rattling the ice in the glass.

"I'm not sure I believe that."

"Why would I lie to you?"

"I don't know." Cage raised a brow. "Why would you? It's a good question. Almost as good as why you would continue to thwart every single attempt at an investigation."

Maurice laughed a bit too loudly. "That's because there's nothing to investigate. Some ex-agent got it into his head that I had something to do with his being burned, so he tried to kill me. And he ended up dead in a flophouse for his trouble. End of story." Maurice tapped the eSlate on his desk and the file on Damian Lasko popped up. "It's all there."

Cage walked over and skimmed through the pages. An image of Lasko appeared and Cage could taste the bile in the back of his throat, remembering the ruined face all melted and hollow on the dirty mattress. The file gave a short chronicle of Lasko's time with MI Six until his sudden departure several years before. Cage tried to click through some of the documents, but many of them had been severely redacted.

"What do you mean 'it's all there?' There's almost no information on him at all."

"That's because there isn't a lot to be had. He was a hacker. An incredibly mediocre agent." Maurice tapped the eSlate again and everything disappeared. "He's dead. Forget it."

"This isn't over," Cage warned.

"It is for me. And seeing as how I get to be the boss around here, it's done for you too, St. John."

Cage could feel his anger rising and he tried to swallow it. Despite Maurice's stubbornness, he had only returned from a major injury days ago. It wouldn't do for him to lose his temper and end up going berserk right here in the office. "Look, Maurice—"

"I mean it, St. John. This is over." Cage started to speak again, but Wilder cut him off. "That's an order."

Cage rolled his eyes and stormed out the door, slamming it behind him. The man had always been an insufferable ass. Cage had grudgingly warmed to him over the last two years given everything he and Phoe had been through. They had known one another in their MI6 days and Cage had thought Wilder was a mealy mouthed accountant who had no place in espionage. But Cage couldn't forget that Maurice had given him a chance to get his old life back when no one else would, and for that, Cage would be forever in his debt.

He emerged from the elevator into Ollie's basement laboratory. Cage remembered Ollie's lab in Machine's compound on New London. This place was much less mad scientist with its shiny white floors and blue-toned florescent lighting. Ollie, Phoe, and Stefan stood around a gurney, staring down at what could only be the remains of the former Mr. Lasko.

"Glad you could grace us with your presence," Ollie said, pointing at the clock. "I thought you said nine."

"I was tied up with Wilder."

"Wilder?" Phoe asked. "What's he doing here?"

"He's a stubborn asshole," Cage replied. "He can't leave the kiddies here with a sitter. We might eat all the candy."

"Or run off trying to catch the guy who tried to kill him." Stefan hit the nail on the head.

"Yeah, he's way less upset about being shot than I would be," Phoe added.

"I'm glad you showed up though," Ollie said. He stood up and threw the sheet over the remains. Cage couldn't help being relieved. He'd seen that thing up close and personal more than enough. He had no desire to see it again. "I have something to show you and Phoe."

Cage and Phoe looked at one another. As the only Ultras at B.E.A.S.T., they often found themselves playing the guinea pigs for all of Ollie's latest gadgets and experiments. "Should we be afraid?"

Ollie smiled and pulled open a drawer. He pulled out what appeared to be a velvet jewelry box. "You two are always complaining that once you've shifted, you can't shift back without being completely naked."

"Yeah," they said in unison.

"The solution is ridiculously simple, but genius. If I do say so myself." He opened the box and showed them two necklaces, each with a small charm. "With a little ingenuity and some miniaturization tech, I've created a way to carry a set of clothes with you." He took one of the necklaces and fastened it around Phoe's neck.

"How is that even possible?" Cage asked, examining his necklace like a strange insect.

"It's quite simple, really," Ollie explained with a wide grin on his face. "It's a suit, with articulated scales."

Phoe touched the necklace and a slick bodysuit unfurled over her body. "Ooh," she gasped. "Neat." She touched it again and the suit was sucked back into the necklace in an instant. "That's too cool," she giggled.

"It's ridiculous," Cage groused. "I'm a spy, not a superhero."

"Why not be both?"

Stefan cleared his throat. "Any way we could forget the fashion show and get back to Lasko? He's still out there, right?"

"Right," Cage answered, shoving the necklace into his pocket. "And Maurice doesn't seem to be worried about that in the least. He claims that Lasko was merely a disgruntled employee."

Stefan scoffed. "Do you believe that?"

"Of course not. Don't be ridiculous. Whoever that was that tried to kill Wilder, it wasn't Damian Lasko."

"Maybe it was," Phoe said. "Maybe someone hired Lasko to pull the trigger and then once the job was done, they killed him. The vampire covens are famous for shit like that. Eliminate the witnesses."

Ollie looked up, nearly blinding them with the light strapped to his forehead. "I like where your head's at, Phoe, but I think it's a bit more complicated." He beckoned them over. "I found something pretty interesting this morning. It's why I called you here." He pulled a large, round magnifying glass down, twisting the metal arm until it was poised over the sheet covering Lasko's body. Cage recoiled. He wasn't sure he needed to see that again, much less close up. "Look here." Ollie grasped a flat, flopping arm from under the sheet and pulled it closer. When no one moved, he groaned in exasperation. "Oh, come on. Don't be wussies."

Phoe leaned closer. Her mouth was screwed up in a disgusted sneer. Remarkably, even then she was gorgeous. "What the hell am I looking at, Ollie?"

Ollie pointed out what looked like tiny bite marks all along the skin of the corpse. "Those, ladies and germs, are the calling card of *parvophalanges.*"

"What in bloody hell are parvophalanges?" Cage asked.

"Literally, the term means 'tiny fingers,' but it describes tiny muscles along the skin of a particular type of Other."

"You think an Other tried to kill Maurice?" Phoe asked.

"No, I think an Other killed Damian Lasko." Ollie turned off his headlamp, pushed the arm back under the sheet, and then took off his gloves as he stepped away from the gurney. He went over to his desk in the corner and rummaged through the mess of papers and books piled high in haphazard disarray. "Have any of you heard the legends about skin walkers?"

"I have," Phoe piped up. "They're legends in many Native American tribes. People that have the ability to turn into animals." She looked pointedly at Cage. "At will."

"Exactly," Ollie stated. "Technically, Cage could be considered a skin walker. But this is something different. According to some legends, wearing the pelt of another animal is what allows the witch to transform." He opened one of his books and showed them a series of illustrations featuring a man wearing a deer skin and antlers transitioning into a stag.

"I don't see the difference." Stefan chuckled.

"Cage is a science experiment," Ollie said. "We sliced and diced the DNA of those creatures and injected a soup of genetic material into our favorite secret agent." He slapped Cage on the shoulder affectionately.

"Thanks," Cage grumbled.

"But this is biological. Messier. Whoever came up with this was getting his DNA from an actual, first-generation Sin'khari."

Stefan began to laugh. "Damian Lasko was a Sin'khari? Come on, Ollie. I think you've been inhaling too many questionable chemicals. The pure species has been gone for millennia."

"Apparently, not Damian," Ollie noted. "As you can see, Damian's skin is lying there on the table."

"You think someone killed Lasko, skinned him alive, and then used his skin as some kind of sicko disguise?" Phoe shook her head. "Even for us that seems a bit farfetched."

"Not necessarily," Ollie said. "Labs all over the world are working with Others, trying to figure out how they tick, and how to harness their strengths. Even the IU, before the serum, tried all kinds of things in an attempt to use the Others for our own gain. Or tried to kill them." He flipped to another photograph showing Maurice's bullet wound. "For example, this. This wound is a perfect example of a slow-kill slug."

"What the hell is that?" Phoe asked.

"It's something that I assumed was still in development. It's a traditional bullet in that it's a missile that one fires out of a gun, but it's been specially designed to kill Others. Once the bullet penetrates the skin, it infects the victim with a slow-acting bacterium that kills the cells."

"So, you rot from the inside out." Cage winced.

"Pretty much."

"It's chemical witchcraft." Phoe scrunched her nose.

"Exactly," Cage said. "And now some of it has gotten out. If Ollie's right, then this thing with Maurice isn't over. It could be just the beginning."

"But it's no use." Stefan shook his head. "Maurice has already ordered that we leave this alone. I understand your concern. I feel it too, but we can't go against our mandate. If Maurice says to forget it, then we need to forget it."

"But why does he want us to forget it?" Phoe asked. "If, in what appears to be out of the blue, I had been nearly killed by some maniac, I'd want someone to catch him."

"Anyone would," Cage agreed. "The fact that Maurice doesn't means that he's hiding something." Cage had known Maurice Wilder for a long time. He had grudgingly befriended him for giving him a chance to get his life back. After all, if it hadn't been for Maurice, Cage would never have met Phoe.

But that didn't mean that Cage fully trusted his boss.

"In my lengthy career," he began, "with MI Six, and now BEAST, I've gotten pretty good at reading people." He strolled over to where an aerial photograph loomed over them. It was almost as if Maurice was here listening. "Everyone thinks guys like Maurice are harmless little weasels hiding in their office. Planning. Plotting. Working within their complicated systems. Never getting their hands dirty, when really their hands are the filthiest of all. They always have secrets, and whatever Maurice's secret is, he's willing to protect it with everything he has at his disposal." He turned to them with an ominous grin. "Even if it means betraying us."

"What do you suggest we do?" Stefan asked. "Right now, all we've got is a hacker pelt and Ollie's mad scientist theories. If you're right, whoever the gunman is, they're long gone by now."

"That's where we start," Phoe said. "We have to find the gunman."

Seven

Two months had passed since the party and everything had remained quiet. Evidently, Maurice had succeeded in sweeping the shooting and Lasko's death under the rug. Which only made Cage more peevish than usual. So much so that Phoe kept putting off telling him about the pregnancy, which somehow, she still carried. She couldn't even wrap her mind around the biology of how she could be pregnant after shifting. The one thing she was sure of: Cage wasn't ready to hear it. It wasn't that she thought he'd be angry or upset, but so much had happened since they had come back from Absinthia, and it all seemed to be moving so fast. On more than one occasion she'd caught him staring into space, as if the whole idea of making her his "official" family had doom written all over it. Add a child into the mix—she feared he'd have an emotional implosion. Now, with everything that had been going on surrounding Maurice's shooting, Cage's anxiety about getting married seemed to be increasing exponentially.

"You do realize that soon, the question of when to tell Cage isn't going to be an issue." Jessica stared at Phoe in the mirror as she buttoned up the back of the wedding dress she was trying on.

"Are you calling me fat?" Phoe asked, absently running a hand over her belly. The satin bodice was pulled tightly across it, clearly showing the outline of the slight bump that was forming. She had never been skin and bones, but the gentle slope of her stomach was becoming noticeably convex.

"No, I'm calling you chicken." Jess chuckled. "Why don't you go ahead and tell him? It'll be one less piece of baggage to carry around."

Phoe sighed. She felt so guilty already, and Jess's constant nagging wasn't helping at all. Phoe had been to see the doctor without him, which was wrong on so many levels. She knew it. She felt guilty about it, and yet, she couldn't get unstuck. So far, she'd been lucky enough to hide her morning sickness, but Jess was right. Soon, the pregnancy was going to be too obvious to hide.

"I know. I know you're right, but… it never seems to be the right time."

"It's possible that he already knows. Cage is pretty perceptive."

"He is, but he's so focused on this thing with the skin walker and Maurice that he barely notices me."

"Stefan told me that Wilder has ordered all of you to forget about the attack and move on with other things."

"He did, but you know how Cage is. Once he gets a bee in his bonnet, he won't stop until he figures it out." Phoe paused and looked over her shoulder at Jess. "Wait… Stef told you that?"

"Well… kind of." Jess blushed. Phoe had known that her sister was quite smitten with the very Viking-like Stefan Mueller, but she wasn't aware that they were close enough to share state secrets.

"Kind of? He isn't supposed to be discussing business with you. You're a civilian."

"Oooh… look who's got an inflated sense of importance," Jess joked. "He isn't telling me lots of secrets about your missions or anything. But we talk."

"I'm sure you do." Phoe couldn't keep the disdain from her tone. While she was glad that Jess had met someone, she wasn't wild to know about their encounters.

"What? I can't talk to my own sister about my dates?"

"Sure you can," Phoe said, turning back to the mirror. "But please leave out the gory details." She stared at herself in the gigantic mirror in the dressing room. "I look like a giant cupcake." The dress that the shopkeeper had brought was a bright white, traditional wedding gown with lace and pearls from head to toe and a train that barely fit in the dressing room.

"Awww… it's pretty."

"No, it's horrendous." Phoe turned as best she could, tugging at the huge bow resting on the bustle. "Whoever decided that brides should wear white was clearly out of their head."

"White is a symbol of innocence. Purity." Jess giggled and squeezed her sister affectionately. "Virginity."

"Yeah well, I haven't been a virgin in quite some time."

"Mom would love you in this dress. You should at least come out to the big mirror and take a look."

"Forget it," Phoe snapped. "The wedding is in six months. In six months, I'll be big as a house, so I need a dress that isn't quite so… fitted."

Jess heaved a put-upon sigh. Phoe almost felt sorry for her sister. She knew she was a terrible shopping companion. Even as a child she'd hated trying on clothes. Until Absinthia, she hadn't ever been able to find clothes that she thought looked right on her body. And with her rapidly changing body, she was even less enthused.

"Mom would come back to haunt me if I let you wear jeans and a t-shirt to your wedding," Jess grumbled.

"I'm not going to wear jeans, but why do I have to wear this ritualistic… sack?"

Jess sighed. "You really hate it?"

"I really do."

Jess rolled her eyes. "Fine. We'll try someplace else."

She helped Phoe get out of the oppressive fabric, but it was no easy task. Yards and yards of unforgiving tulle and satin made her feel claustrophobic as she fought her way free. In her two years as an agent, she'd never been in so vicious a trap. Finally, Jess was able to pull Phoe free of the dress.

When the two women exited the dressing room, Phoe handed the dress over to the saleslady, who seemed slightly insulted that Phoe hadn't been able to find the dress of her dreams, but she didn't much care.

As they stood there, Jess arguing with the woman over sizing, Phoe noticed a man staring at them out of the corner of her eye. He was dressed in a gray suit with no tie—well-tailored, with perfect hair. He sat in one of the seating areas across the room with the other fathers, trying not to look as if he were watching them. Girls would come out of the room and he would smile, but he never spoke. It was an old spy trick, blending into another group.

"What is it?" Jess asked, tugging at Phoe's arm. She followed Phoe's gaze to where the man sat staring.

"Look at that man."

Jess grinned. "Hmm… cute."

"I wasn't asking for an opinion on his physical characteristics."

"Well why else would you be watching him?"

"I think that man is watching *us*," Phoe whispered.

"Why would you think that?

"He hasn't taken his eyes off us since we got here. I thought he was with that group, but he hasn't moved. When we went into the dressing room, there was another group of girls trying on wedding dresses. But those are different girls trying on bridesmaids' dresses. That guy is still there."

"Eew." Jess pulled a face. "Do you think he's a pervert who hangs out at ladies' dressing rooms?"

Phoe shook her head. "I'm not sure. Come to think of it, I think I saw him in the last place we went."

"You think he's following us?" Jess asked, her voice climbing in volume.

"Shush," Phoe hissed. "I don't know, but I think we should get out of here."

They walked out the door and made their way down the street and around the corner to another bridal shop. It was an unusually sunny day in London, and Phoe was relieved. She'd invited Jess to come to stay with her and Cage for a few weeks to get the bulk of the wedding plans done, but it had rained steadily since the day Jess had arrived a week ago. It made wandering around the shopping district near their flat pretty difficult.

"You know, I think that working at BEAST is making you paranoid," Jess told her as they crossed the street.

"What do you mean?"

"I mean, that poor man back there was probably waiting for his daughter to come out of the dressing room."

Phoe shrugged. "Maybe. I still think he was suspicious."

When they walked into the bridal shop across the road, Phoe knew immediately that this was much more in keeping with her own style. The shop was tiny, with a single large mirror and platform. No spotlights or posh salespeople in tailored suits. And not a single cupcake dress in sight.

"Dear God, it's like the crunchy granola hippie bride shop," Jess snarked.

"I know. Isn't it great?"

"Hello," a cheerful voice called from behind them. "Welcome to Something Old, London's only vintage bridal shop."

Phoe turned and smiled, seeing a round woman with mounds of curly blonde hair. "Oh, hi. We, uh, don't have an appointment."

"You don't need one," she replied. "We like to keep things pretty chill around here." She pulled off her tiny reading glasses and swept them on top of her head, staring at the two women. "So, which one of you is the bride?"

"I am," Phoe said. "And I don't want to look like a cupcake."

The woman giggled. "I completely understand." She regarded Jess, narrowing her eyes and she stared up and down her frame. "And you must be the maid of honor?"

"I am. I mean, I'm her sister, so…"

"Great." The woman took their coats and purses and hung them on a rack behind the counter. "Come on. Let's pick out some dresses to try." Phoe looked over her shoulder at Jess with a reluctant glare. The salesgirl paused and snapped her fingers at Jess. "You too. While I'm helping—?"

"Phoebe. I mean, Phoe."

"While I'm helping Phoe into the first dress, you can get started looking at these books." She motioned for Jess to sit down on the chaise in front of the modeling platform. A pile of fashion books was sitting on the coffee table.

Phoe didn't have time to protest as the woman led her through the store, past racks upon racks of vintage style dresses. "Uhm… I haven't really picked anything out yet."

"Of course, you haven't," the woman stated as she threw aside the curtain to an oversized fitting room. "I'll bring one of each style. You'll try them on and see which one you like best, then we can worry about finding the perfect dress." She stood back and sized Phoe up. "You're what, about a ten US?"

"A twelve, but how did you know that?"

"It's my job to know, love." The woman paused and stood back, eyeing Phoe up and down. A small grin lit up her face. "When's the baby due?"

Phoe gasped. "God, is it that obvious?"

"No, but as I said, I have a sort of sixth sense about things. So, when's the baby due?"

"Seven months."

The saleslady giggled. "Oh well, then we'll need to go Regency. High waistlines, flowing fabric." She tapped her fingernails against her teeth, deep in thought. "Actually, I think I have something perfect." She offered Phoe a wink and threw the curtain closed and rushed into the aisles, leaving Phoe alone to strip.

She stared at herself in the mirror as she pulled her clothes off. Was her pregnancy already so obvious? Her time as an agent had toned her body, but not overly so. She was still curvaceous and soft. For the first time in her life, she was okay with that. Cage never missed an opportunity to tell her how beautiful she was, how much he loved the softness of her bosom, or how the generous curve of her hips seemed to fit perfectly against his. He'd given her a confidence that she'd wished for throughout her life. Now, she hoped that he would be as accepting of this new body.

She had to admit that she could see herself changing. Her breasts were pushing against the fabric of her bra. Soon they'd be spilling over. Her belly was rounding and she could swear that her hips were wider.

Then there was the small, faded scar over the waistband of her underwear. So small that no one would ever notice it. Except Phoe. Every time she looked in the mirror, her eyes immediately locked on that scar. Cage had asked her about it several times, but she'd said she didn't really remember how it happened. Some ancient childhood accident that she guessed had been blocked out.

But that wasn't true.

The source of that scar was the only secret that remained between them. She wasn't sure why she'd never told him. Much like her pregnancy, she had tried so many times, but she couldn't seem to find the right words. Was she afraid he would think her weak? That she'd gotten so frightened she had run away from New Orleans because she was a scaredy cat? Or maybe she was afraid of that herself. Phoe knew there was no room in a family for secrets. She would have to tell him soon.

"All right, Phoebe," the saleslady called from outside the dressing room. "I brought a few different sizes since you don't have a foundation garment today."

Ten minutes later, Phoe emerged from the dressing room wearing the first gown. She wasn't wild about the design, but the style was fantastic. The dress wasn't long or bulky. It was exactly the kind of thing she had been looking for. The bodice was a simple ivory satin with only a little embellishment, save for a sash under the bust. Layers of tulle fell from the high waist to slightly above the knee.

"Isn't this amazing?" she asked, twirling around for Jess.

Jess scrunched her nose up. "Maybe if you were dancing in a cage with white boots."

"What do you mean?"

"I mean, that dress isn't exactly... bridal."

Phoe rolled her eyes. "Oh my God, really? You've spent most of your adult life flying around in outer space and now you've decided to be a prude?"

Jess shrugged. "I dunno. Maybe I can hear Mom's voice in my head. She'd have a cow if she saw you wearing that at your wedding."

"Well then it's a good thing she won't be there..." Phoe's words trailed off as she noticed the door across the room open. The man in the gray suit walked in, his eyes shifting back and forth as if he were looking for something.

"That's kind of a shitty thing to say, Sis."

Suddenly, the man's eyes locked with Phoe's. He held her gaze for a long moment and then turned to dart back out the door.

"Wait," Phoe shouted, stepping down off the platform. "Stop that man."

"Who?" Jess asked, looking around.

The saleslady came out of the back and Phoe nearly bowled her over as she took off after him. "Miss, what are you doing?" she called. "You have to pay for the dress."

Phoe blocked out the voices shouting her name. She had zeroed in on the man and she wasn't going to let him get away. He knew something. She darted between pedestrians as she ran after him. He looked over his shoulder, noticing that she was following him, and he sped up, diving into the onslaught of pedestrians on the sidewalk. As if something was controlling them, they seemed to huddle around the man, creating a barrier between him and Phoe. She tried to fight her way through, shoving her arms between theirs and pushing them aside. One lady tumbled off the sidewalk and into the street, but Phoe didn't stop. The man darted in front of a cab and across the street, and Phoe followed.

The guy turned a corner and ran down an alley. As soon as she was off the street, Phoe called the phoenix and burst into the firebird in an instant. She shot straight up into the air, screeching loudly. The noise bounced off the walls of the buildings, which made the cry sound as if she were coming from all directions at once. She heard the gray man whine, covering his ears as he stumbled over some boxes lying on the ground. He looked back and screamed as Phoe dove toward him, her talons fully extended.

"What the fuck are you?" he screamed. He swept his arms over his head, batting her away.

She dodged his blows easily. She needed to get him out of here. Somewhere hidden where she could question him. She screeched again and this time he fell down on his knees, holding the sides of his head. The scream of the phoenix was painful to the human ear and she had learned to wield her voice as a weapon. As soon as he fell, she was on top of him, tearing at his clothes with her claws, trying to get him in her grasp.

Without warning, the man's arm shot up and he grabbed Phoe out of the sky. She squawked as he grabbed her tail feathers and he screamed when he threw her to the asphalt. Her body was unfathomably hot. When he held her to the ground, she could smell his flesh burning. She tried to turn her body, to use her strength to break away, but he held her in such a way that she could not gain purchase.

"Hey," a woman's voice shouted.

Phoe craned her neck toward the voice. Jess was standing at the head of the alley. She held a walking cane in front of her like a bat. Phoe had to hand it to her. She might not know a thing about fighting, but she sure as hell knew how to look absolutely insane. She let out a battle cry as she rushed toward them, swiping at the air with her cane. "You get the fuck off my sister, you bastard."

The man's eyes were like dinner plates as she lit upon him like a woman possessed. She pummeled him about the head and shoulders with the aluminum cane until he stumbled backward and crawled out of her reach. Phoe tried to raise up but found that she could barely move. She screeched one more time and then burst into flames at the same time the man took off down the alley.

Jess rushed to her sister's side. "Phoe, are you okay?"

Phoe groaned in response as her ashen body became solid and melted back to its natural form. "Ugh... no." She was relieved to find that she was still wearing Ollie's clever necklace. She pressed the charm and a black bodysuit grew from her neck down over her body in slick scales that shifted and arranged themselves. Jess hesitated, then pulled her sister to an upright position.

"That asshole tried to kill me."

"I think he was fighting for his life," Jess said with a chuckle. "I can't blame him. You were pretty frightening." Jess's voice sounded miles away.

After a shift, Phoe always felt sore and a little nauseated, but this was different. She could hear the blood rushing through her veins and her muscles jerked and trembled. Her body felt hot, but she was shivering. "Jess," she gasped. "I uh… I don't feel so well."

"Well that's understandable. You turned into a giant firebird and then burst into flames while your body put itself back together."

"No… really…" Phoe grabbed Jess's arm. "I think I should see the doctor." Her voice trembled. "The baby…"

Eight

Cage thought that giant gerbils on wheels must have been powering the incredibly slow elevator at Queen's Hospital. He tapped his foot incessantly as he watched the lights go up. Three, four, five... at each floor he tensed, hoping that the carriage wasn't going to stop to let more people on. He had to get to Phoe.

Jessica had called and told him she was taking Phoe to the hospital in a cab. She hadn't said why they were going, but judging by the tone of her voice, it was an emergency. He wanted to kick himself. He shouldn't have let her go with Jess this morning. He should have insisted Phoe stay home and rest. The last couple of weeks, she had seemed run down. He'd woken up to her vomiting several mornings. Evidently, the stress of their impending marriage was catching up to her. Not to mention that he hadn't been a joy to live with. This thing with Wilder was troubling him and making him more irascible than usual.

The doors finally opened, and Cage burst into the emergency wing. The look on his face must have been particularly frightening because the nurses in the hall turned their back and hurried off.

"Excuse me," he called, rapping on the counter at the nurses' station. "Can I get some help please?" A nurse on the phone put a silencing finger up and pushed a clipboard in his direction. He looked down at it like he didn't understand this odd device. "Miss... Miss... I don't think you heard me."

The nurse rolled her eyes and tapped the earpiece she was talking into. "Sir, you'll need to fill out these forms and have a seat in the waiting area."

"No, I'm not filling out any forms or waiting. My fiancée is here, and I need to see her."

"All right, sir. But you'll have to have a seat. Someone will be with you shortly."

Cage could feel the all too familiar rage bubbling under his skin. This woman had no idea how close she was skating to total annihilation. "I realize that you're trying to do your job, but—"

"If you'll just sit—"

"I'm not sitting down," Cage shouted, slamming his fist down on the counter so hard that it left a divot.

"Hey, slugger." Jess jogged up the hall, pulling Cage away from the nurses' station before he ended up on the news. "Come this way. Phoe's in a room."

Cage followed Jess down the hall. "What in hell happened? Is she all right?"

"Yes, she's fine. We were out shopping for dresses. She kept seeing this guy and she thought he was following us."

"Who?"

"No idea. Some guy wearing a gray suit. And I must admit that it was kind of weird the way he kept showing up. At the last store we were in, she saw him and took off after him." Jess looked around and lowered her voice to barely a whisper as they reached the room. "She shifted and went after him."

When he got to the doorway of the room and saw Phoe, his heart clenched. She was sitting atop a hospital bed, leaned back while a doctor listened to her heartbeat. Cage shoved Jess out of the way and barreled into the room. "Phoe, are you all right?"

"Cage, hi." She half-waved as if nothing much was going on. "What are you doing here?"

"You're my fiancée and you're in the hospital. Where else should I be?"

She offered a nervous smile, then looked past him toward Jess. "I told you not to call him."

"Sorry, sis. I thought he should be here."

Phoe closed her eyes, heaving a heavy sigh. "Cage, I'm fine. This is Doctor Desjardins."

Cage offered his hand. "Is she all right?"

"Right as rain," Dr. Desjardins said. "A little overexertion."

"Overexertion?" Cage asked, turning to Jess. "What in hell were you doing? I thought you were going to try on wedding dresses."

"We were. We did…"

"Miss Addison," Dr. Desjardins admonished. "A woman in your condition shouldn't be running after a purse snatcher."

"A purse snatcher?" Cage pushed past Desjardins and knelt by Phoe's bed. "Don't tell me you were running after some wanker purse snatcher. Did he have a gun?"

"No," Phoe answered. "It was fine."

"It wasn't fine. What if he'd had a weapon? He could have hurt you or Jess. Trust me, nothing in your purse was worth that."

"I think I could handle one little punk kid," Phoe stated.

"Your fiancé is right, Miss Addison," Desjardins said. "Best not to risk it. This early in your pregnancy, it would be wise to be cautious."

"You and I both know that there's never just one punk kid…" Cage's voice trailed off as he slowly processed what the doctor had said. He turned to look at the doctor. "Wait. Say that again."

"Miss Addison is pregnant. She needs to take it easy."

He whipped around. Phoe started to say something, but instead looked away, hiding her face in her hands.

"Good job, Doc," Jess muttered.

"At any rate, Miss Addison is fine. She'll need to go home and rest tonight, but I think by the morning she'll be fine." He looked from Phoe to Cage, neither of them speaking. "Uh… you might want to follow up with your… uhm… obstetrician. This week."

"Thank you, Doctor," Jess said, trying to steer him from the room. "I'll be sure that she rests."

"I assumed he knew."

"Of course, Doc." Jess practically shoved him out the door and closed it behind them.

For several seconds, neither of them spoke. The silence was heavy. Cage felt like his brain was malfunctioning. Emotions he didn't even know he had were tumbling around, getting mixed up together. Surprise, fear, anger, and unequivocal happiness—they all fired simultaneously in his mind until all he could say was, "Are you sure?"

Phoe nodded. "Positive."

"Did… did the doctor do like… a test or something when you came in?" Suddenly, his body felt too heavy and he sat down on the edge of the bed.

"No. They asked me a bunch of questions when we came in. I thought I'd better tell them. In case, you know?"

"So, you knew before."

Phoe nodded, avoiding his eyes.

"How long?"

"Since the party. I did a test that morning."

Cage's eyes were like saucers, and when he stood up, he stumbled over his feet. "Before the party? What, the engagement party?"

"Yes…"

"Two months ago?"

"Cage, please. Don't go crazy."

"Me? I'm crazy? You're the one hiding this pregnancy from me, but I'm crazy."

"I'm not hiding it from you. I've tried to tell you a thousand times."

"Am I that hard to talk to?"

"No, but… this is different. I know how hard this wedding stuff has been for you. I know that it makes you think about Corinne and Lily. I didn't want to add to your anxiety."

"God, Phoe," Cage sighed, getting up and starting to pace around the room. "You make me sound like a nervous old lady."

"You know that's not what I meant," Phoe countered. "But I didn't know how you would react and I guess maybe I was a little afraid to find out."

Cage was shocked. Could it really be that his Phoe was afraid to talk to him? He knew that he wasn't always the easiest person to talk to. He had a temper. It was true, but he tried to keep it in check these days. Especially with her.

"I don't know what to say. Am I really such a beast?"

"Of course, you're not a beast. Far from it. But I—I didn't want you to feel… trapped."

"How would I feel trapped?"

She shrugged. "I know that our getting married wasn't where you saw our relationship going."

"That's not true."

"Oh yes, it is. You said so yourself."

"Well, maybe it used to be true, but I do want to marry you. I wouldn't have asked if I didn't."

"I know," she mumbled, her cheeks ripening to a pink glow. "But I don't want you to think that I got pregnant to keep you in this relationship. To force you to go through with the marriage."

Cage took her hand and squeezed it gently. "God, Phoe. I would never think that. And any apprehension I might have about our getting married or having a child has nothing to do with not wanting to." He slid higher on the bed and turned, pulling her close to him. "You are everything I've ever wanted, and you having our child makes me explode with love for you even more."

She laughed and leaned into his embrace. "That sounds so damn sappy coming from you."

"I know, right? I can't believe it myself. But it's true." He brushed his fingers through her hair and cupped her cheek. He stared down into her eyes, seeing a sparkle of happiness. He brushed a gentle kiss over her mouth. "Phoebe Addison, I'm going to make you and our baby so happy."

She nestled into his chest, wrapping her arms around him. He felt her body relax into his embrace as if some incredible weight had been lifted from her shoulders. "Silly boy. I already am."

They lay there together for some time. Neither of them spoke, but they didn't have to. They had a communication that transcended all words as they watched the sun slip down below the horizon.

Eventually, Cage could hear her breathing even out. She slept. Poor thing was exhausted. He remembered how tired Corinne had been at the beginning of her pregnancy with Lily. He could only imagine the strength Phoe had called upon to chase whomever that was. The doctor had assured him that she was all right, but he was going to make Ollie take a look. They really had no idea how the Splice would affect this pregnancy.

But something else bothered him. It wasn't like Phoe to be paranoid. The man in the gray suit that she thought was following her—who was it? A knot in his gut made him think that whoever it was, he had something to do with the attempted assassination of Wilder.

Cage was certain of one thing: whoever that bloody man was, they needed to find him.

Nine

Cage stood under the shower, a steady stream of water pouring down over his aching head. It had been three days since Phoe's incident and Cage was about to go out of his mind. Not only was he sick of being cooped up, but Wilder had temporarily benched them. Apparently Phoe's delicate condition had gotten back to the powers that be. Never mind the fact that she was as tough as she always had been, Wilder had assigned them to a mountain of paperwork. No doubt thrilled they were forced to do deskwork.

Ollie hadn't been much help. The day after, he'd examined Phoe and determined that while her shift hadn't adversely affected their baby, that she really ought to take it easy for a while. It was a diagnosis that she heartily resented. The last seventy-two hours had been a constant struggle to keep her off her feet.

And then there was the thirst.

Ever since Cage first took the Splice, Ollie had been trying to figure out a way to make a perfect synthetic blood for him. He'd come close. The gooey, vitamin-rich liquid had all the nutrients that he required to keep himself strong, even in daylight, and he didn't have to hunt. Of course, it was like a person on a diet eating meal replacements. It had all the essential vitamins, but it wasn't quite the same. Real, human blood was the only thing that truly satisfied him, and his supply was nearly gone. Tonight, as much as he loathed the idea, he'd resolved to venture into Whitechapel to a little dive Stefan had told him about called Death's Door.

Cage pulled on a pair of black trousers and a close-fitting button-up and tie to match. His hair was still wet, and he combed it back in a slick style that screamed Bela Lugosi. Looking at himself in the mirror, Cage thought he looked like Satan's valet, but the stereotype would work to his advantage tonight.

After checking to make sure that Phoe was still asleep, he slipped down the stairs. He didn't want to go, but extreme situations called for extreme measures. Not to mention that while he'd done his best to adapt to her human schedule, Cage found it difficult to sleep at night. Times like this, he was acutely aware that the base DNA of his Splice was that of a vampire.

The Whitechapel district in London was famous for being the site of the Ripper killings in the late nineteenth century, and in truth, it hadn't changed all that much. True, some gentrification was evident, prettied up by corporate buyers, but the black heart of the little hamlet remained firmly intact.

A turn off the High Street, and Cage was plunged into a labyrinth of narrow streets and dark corners. In one of those corners was Death's Door. At one time, it had been an old slaughterhouse. In fact, most of the décor was antique meat hooks and knives. The perfect place for a secret vampire club.

Cage could smell the blood before he made it through the front door. He was expecting to see a line of bodies hanging from the ceiling, dripping all their sanguine goodness down onto the dancers on the floor. The thought made his mouth water.

"Oy, mate. Members only." The oversized bouncer sat on a stool up ahead, waving people inside. He was clearly not a vampire. His eyebrows were bushy, and his teeth had slight points. Werewolf, Cage thought. He was surprised to see so many humans in the line to get inside. When they reached the bouncer, they pulled their collars down or rolled up their sleeves to show their membership badges: two tiny, bleeding wounds—the sign of a babydoll.

The babydoll culture—the term "babydoll" referred to the glassy gaze of a human tasting vampire blood—was a phenomenon that accompanied the rise of the vampire covens on Earth. Most vampire groupies offered their blood freely in exchange for a small taste of vampire blood, which offered healing and vitality. It wasn't a high, per se, but a drop of vampire blood could cure minor illnesses, heal wounds, and gave a feeling of robust youth. But others were greedier. They wanted to be turned.

The thought of taking advantage of such an abhorrent practice was sickening, but Cage was desperate. He'd promised Phoe that he wouldn't hunt unless he had to. And he didn't miss it much. One of the vampiric traits that proved useful was the touch telepathy, but also the most exhausting. With one touch, a vampire could see straight into the mind of his meal and learn the dark secrets, desperate yearnings, and hidden desires that were displayed for a hunting vampire. He supposed the talent was supposed to be used in order to find weaknesses, but Cage had resolved years ago not to feast on innocent blood. He used the link to make that determination.

When Cage approached the bouncer, he felt the smug confidence dissipate in a wave of body odor. "Members only, mate," he croaked, trying not to look Cage in the eye. He knew Cage was a vampire.

Cage flashed his eyes. "Proof enough, mate?" he asked, giving the bare glimpse of his fangs.

The bouncer nodded quickly and opened the rope gate. Cage couldn't help smiling. He had to admit to the tiniest twinge of pleasure at inciting fear that way. That twinge could very well be the most addictive part of being a vampire. That rush of power, knowing that you could make a total stranger do whatever you wanted. It was exhilarating. From that perspective, Cage could understand why there were so many acolytes begging for attention.

Death's Door was a small, sweaty nightclub. There was a microscopic dancefloor where couples moved slowly to the lazy beat of strange music the likes of which could be heard nowhere else. There was a bar, of course, but most of the patrons were sitting in the dark booths or draped over one another on the ragged couches and chaises that were arranged haphazardly around the room. The darkness was broken only by the milky light of a single chandelier overhead and a few oil lamps, which hung in sconces along the walls.

Cage coughed as he made his way to the bar. It smelled like vampires. The coppery scent of blood underscored by the sickly sweetness of opium. The walls were stained with brown splatters that could be left over from an overenthusiastic butcher—or, more likely, from last night's crowd.

He sat down at a barstool and nodded to the bartender. The man immediately set a goblet in front of him and poured a generous glass of Animus—animal blood mixed with wine and a cocktail of vitamins. It was supposed to be more like the real thing, but Cage thought the flavor still fell flat. They also kept it cold so that the blood stayed fresh. He downed it quickly, trying to avoid tasting it.

"That shit's disgusting, don't you think?"

Cage turned as a thin boy in a trim, velvet suit slid onto the stool beside him. His hair, dyed a purplish black, hung down over a pair of violet eyes that had obviously been enhanced. The dim light cast shadows over the boy's face. That, coupled with the deathly pallor, made him appear almost skeletal. Cage stifled a laugh.

"I suppose beggars can't be choosers," Cage replied, waving for the bartender to bring another glass.

"So they say," the boy drawled. He pulled a gold case from his jacket. With a flick of his thumb, it popped open and the boy pulled out a long, clove cigarette. He didn't offer Cage one but pressed it between his lips and gazed at him expectantly.

Going into his pocket, Cage fished out a silver lighter and clicked it open. The boy leaned in, hovering the end of his cigarette over the tiny blue flame, then pursed his lips in a perfect O as he sucked in the smoke. His eyes never left Cage's.

"So, what brings you to Death's Door?"

Cage gave a mirthless chuckle and took another sip of the Animus. "The Plague."

The boy blew a thin plume of spicy smoke over their heads. "Sounds serious."

"Only if you don't know the cure."

Cage stared across the bar to where a couple of female vampires reclined on a chaise with a woman. The vampires were exquisite. If they were drones, then they were old. Only those directly descended from the Sin'khari were so flawless. One had deep black hair that lay straight and silken across her shoulders. Her red lips were the same color as the blood that ran from one corner. The other was a curvaceous redhead with large, buoyant curls that bounced around a pair of playful eyes. Their beauty only highlighted the rundown, sallow form of the woman between them. She lay there, unmoving as they slithered around her. Wounds in her wrists and the insides of her elbows dribbled blood slowly down her arms, thinned by their venom. Her clothes were stained with it, but the woman didn't seem to notice. Her eyes were glazed and unfocused, like most babydolls, but this was something more.

"Don't worry, mate. They won't do her in."

Cage started. He'd forgotten that the boy sat beside him. "Of course not," he said. "She's a babydoll."

"Worse," the boy replied. "She's one of the afflicted."

"Afflicted."

"It used to be the Gift she was after. Now E is all she loves."

"E?"

The boy nodded to the scene. The vampires whispered softly to the woman. They lapped at her wounds, sharing her blood between them, licking each other's lips until their mouths were smeared scarlet stains. They painted a tableau that was both erotic and disturbing. The redhead pulled a vial on a chain from her bodice. She dangled it between her fingers over the woman. Immediately her eyes sparked and she raised up, almost panting. The dark one shushed her, kissing the soft spot beside her ear.

"Please," the woman begged. "Just a little. I've been good."

"Careful, love. Not so much." The redhead opened the vial and poured a tiny drop over the woman's open mouth. Cage followed the drop from the lip of the bottle to where it dribbled over the woman's chin. She lapped it up with her tongue, whimpering. Her eyes implored them to give her more, but the vampires only laughed.

"Such a pretty plaything." Suddenly, whatever they gave her began to take hold. Her body relaxed, and her eyes closed. She lay back against the chaise as the vampires petted and soothed her. "There now, love. All better now."

The boy chuckled and put out the end of his cigarette beside Cage. "One drop is all it takes. Now she'll let them do anything they like. Up to and including killing her. Silly whore."

Cage stared at them, unable to pull his eyes away. The vampires used their nails to slice open the side of the woman's neck. The wounds at her wrists and arms oozed slowly. That was where he'd bitten Phoe a few times. Most places on the body, the veins were close to the surface, and while they bled, the prey was not in danger. The neck and groin were the sweet spots. A vampire could drain a human from a neck wound in seconds, and from the groin in even less time. No babydoll would allow her host to drink from her jugular vein unless she was drugged.

"They'll kill her," Cage muttered, starting up off his stool.

"No, they won't," the boy said, placing a calming hand on Cage's shoulder. "They'll leave her alive. She's far more delicious that way."

Cage turned, and the boy grinned. Those enormous, round eyes and sharp bone structure robbed the boy's face of any humor. In fact, his expression gave Cage a chill. "How can you be sure?"

"She does it every night. She's addicted to the *eshar*." The boy's fingertips slid down Cage's arm and across his hand. He stroked the bones at the back in a way that instantly made Cage jerk it away. "What about you, Mr. St. John? Looking for a top-off tonight?" The boy inhaled deeply. He closed his eyes as if breathing Cage in was a sacred ceremony. "You smell hungry, *khari-ma*."

Khari-ma was the word for a vampire born of the Sin'khari. Cage was somewhat flattered that this boy assumed he was of such exquisite stock. That was probably the point.

"I'm far too dangerous for you, boy," Cage said, backing away. Then it dawned on him. "Wait... how did—?"

"How did I know your name?" The boy sat back on his stool, staring up at the ceiling. "Maybe a little bird told me."

"A bird. I find that hard to believe."

Out of the corner of his eye, he caught a slight movement. He grabbed the boy's hand and slammed it down on the bar, banging the wrist hard. The boy shrieked, drawing the attention of the whole place. A syringe rolled down the bar and onto the floor. Cage bared his teeth and growled low at the boy. "Who the fuck are you and what do you want?"

"Be cool, mate. We don't want to draw attention—"

Cage stood up and in a swift movement twisted the boy's arm behind his back. He could hear the bones crack. The bouncer from the front walked inside the doorway, but when Cage flashed his eyes, he backed down. Everyone was frozen, waiting to see what would happen next. Even the vampires with the *eshar* junkie looked up. Cage dared anyone to say anything as he walked the boy across the bar and out the door.

When they reached the alley, Cage released the boy and shoved him hard to the ground.

"Take it easy, man."

"You better start talking, asshole." The kid skidded in the gravel as he tried to gain footing, but Cage shoved him back down in the mud with a firm boot to the kid's ass. "Who are you? Were you the one following Phoe?"

"What? I don't know what you're talking about."

"How did you know my name?" Cage reached down and grabbed the kid before he could stand up and threw him against the brick wall.

"All right," the kid exclaimed, putting his hands up in surrender. "Just… let me…" He wiped blood from his lip and held out his hand. "Here… do you want the blood?"

"I'm going to have considerably more than a handful if you don't tell me how the fuck you know me." He started toward the kid again when he heard the distinctive sound of an autopistol safety click behind him.

"Not one more step, St. John. You might be able to heal, but I bet I could splatter your brains pretty painfully over that asphalt."

Cage looked up at the kid, who shrugged. He turned into the barrel of the pistol in his face. A large werebeast in a suit snarled at him. Cage could hear the hum of the mechanism inside the autopistol, getting ready to fire. "What do you want?"

"Let's go for a ride, Mr. St. John. There's someone waiting for you."

"Who?"

"Never mind that now." A black prowler dropped down in the alley ahead and stopped. "Your ride's here."

Cage hesitated and the werebeast waved him forward. Cage could probably shift and get out of this, but who was to say that if he didn't go with whomever this was that they wouldn't go after Phoe?

Besides, now he was kind of curious.

Ten

The whole scenario would have been hilarious if it weren't so inconvenient. The walking cliché and his beefy driver had insisted that Cage wear an earpiece that impeded his ability to shift through a high-frequency wave. He'd reluctantly agreed but sent a signal to Phoe via his commlink as he climbed into the back of the prowler. Just in case.

They drove across the bridge and out into the countryside. The lights of London were soon far behind, making Cage feel completely isolated. He glanced up at the dashboard of the prowler and noticed the time. He'd been gone several hours. Phoe would be worried when she got his coordinates. He could also feel the sharp fangs cutting at his gums. He still hadn't eaten, and his body was starting to rebel. If he didn't have something soon, it was likely that his companions would end up being casualties.

The kid sat opposite him, silently fiddling with the cuff of his jacket. Funny, he'd been pretty chatty at the club before.

"So, if I asked who sent you, would you tell me?"

"Of course not," the kid answered.

"But you have been following me?"

"Only tonight."

Cage nodded. "You weren't following Phoe?"

"I don't have any idea who that is, but I'm going to go with no. Only you." The kid winked and pulled out another clove cigarette. He didn't light it but rolled it between his fingers. Obviously nervous. Cage thought the kid might be able to have fun with this.

"Relax, Mr. St. John. All will be revealed."

If he wasn't so curious, Cage thought he might be handing this guy his lungs. He really didn't like being toyed with. He started to reach into his pocket for his eSlate. "Oy, mate. Don't do that." He laid a hand on his hip and Cage could see the definite outline of an autopistol. "We're almost there."

The prowler set down at the head of a gravel path that led through a thicket of trees. The moonlight barely broke through the canopy as they moved slowly through the woods. When they reached a clearing, a dilapidated manor house rose up before them. Crumbling bricks and broken windows were highlighted by a curtain of ivy. When the vehicle came to a stop, the driver jerked the door open.

Cage never broke eye contact with the beast as he stood up. The driver let out a low growl. Cage responded, flashing his vampire eyes and baring his fangs.

"Come, Mr. St. John," the kid said, pulling slightly at his shoulder. "My employer doesn't like to be kept waiting."

The front doors reached high above them. They were made of heavy oak planks held together with iron rivets. The kid had to push hard to get through. Cage was almost expecting Count Dracula himself to greet them in the foyer, but no such luck. Only a crumbling staircase.

"How very Mary Shelley," Cage commented as he followed the kid inside. Decayed grandeur was the only way to describe it. Moth-eaten tapestries hung from the walls. The planks under their feet creaked with every step. A strange light shone from above, and when he looked up, Cage realized that there were chinks in the walls and ceiling where moonlight streamed through. "I can't wait to see Dr. Frankenstein's laboratory."

"This way." The kid gestured toward a sitting room. Cage strolled inside, his gaze searching everywhere. While he had no doubt that he could overpower the kid and the driver if he had to, there was no telling what kind of horror might be lurking in the dark corners of this place.

The room was bare. There was a stained table that looked like it would tip over at any moment, and two straight-backed chairs arranged on either side. Evidently, this place was abandoned, and someone was using it as a squat. A place where one could easily dispose of another if the occasion arose.

Cage touched the device that had been clipped around his ear. He tugged at it, thinking that perhaps there was a way to snap the device off, but he only succeeded in nearly deafening himself with a high-pitched squeal. Oh well. If this went badly, he'd have to resort to brute force. And if all else failed, Phoe had the coordinates of his position, and B.E.A.S.T. could be here within minutes, if need be. He wondered if his captor knew about the commlink.

There was an odd whirring sound and Cage turned, taking an attack position. The kid stood by the doorway, unmoving as someone, or something, made its way down the hall and into the sitting room.

"Mr. St. John, I'm so glad you could join me."

The voice was familiar. Immediately, the urge to shift began to burn under Cage's skin. His fangs breached the thin skin at his gum line and his breath was short. Unfortunately, that annoying buzz from the earpiece kept him still.

"Now I understand the inhibitor," Cage said through clenched teeth.

Derek Machine stepped from the shadowy doorway and lurched toward the sitting room. He was painfully thin and even paler than Cage remembered. He seemed stretched. For a man who had spent his life devouring innocents, Machine looked almost puny. When he turned, one half of his face was marred by a mask of wrinkly skin that was nearly transparent. "Well, I had to protect myself, didn't I?"

When he sat down, Cage could see the source of the whirring. One of Machine's arms and his lower half was almost completely mechanical. A red gleam from a cybernetic eye scanned Cage.

"Forgive me, mate, but you look a bit worse for wear. I thought that you had escaped from your exploits relatively unscathed."

"Oh, you mean this?" He pointed at the eye. "A parting gift from you and your blushing bride. I suppose I can't blame you for loving her. She's exactly the kind of psychopath that normally falls for you. Anyhow, you're right. I did manage to escape from the roof of my mansion in New London. But of course, that lovely fire and explosion the two of you caused by setting those beasts free—let's say that 'escape' is a relative term."

"I wish I could *say* I was sorry to hear it."

Machine shrugged, barking another watery cough into his handkerchief. "The explosion caused my helicopter to crash. My pilot was killed instantly, but I got to lie in the courtyard, barely breathing, long enough for Manning's test subjects to chew on me a bit." He pulled a flask from his lapel and took a generous swig of whatever was inside. The sound of it going down his throat made Cage's stomach turn. "But I'm not bitter." Machine cleared his throat and waved his hand at the kid who still stood by the doorway. "But my congratulations on your pending nuptials. I do hope it goes better than last time."

"How did you know about…?"

"How couldn't I? It isn't hard to find information about you, St. John. You can't seem to keep a low profile."

Cage sighed, yawning as he paced around the room. "So, what's this about, then? Revenge? I mean, if you'd wanted to kill me, I've given you ample opportunity. Perhaps you'd like to give us a wedding gift?"

A grinding, watery sound came from Machine as he laughed. He must have some biomech inside as well, Cage thought. Whatever happened to Machine in New London was far worse than anything the IU could have imposed.

"It's true that for a while I fantasized about disemboweling you both slowly with a pair of rusted scissors. Or perhaps blinding her with a hot blade as efficiently as she did to poor Eve Manning. Especially when infection took my legs and a portion of my intestine. In fact, wreaking vengeance upon you and your pet is the only thought that's kept me going these last few years."

Cage clenched both fists at his sides. He was painfully aware that he'd willingly walked into a trap. "You can't be waiting for me to apologize."

Machine grinned, straightening his mechanical leg and loosening a valve. A stinking plume of chemical steam hissed out. "I know that remorse would be too much to ask from a man like you. It isn't in your nature."

"Oh?"

"Don't think I'm insulting you, Macijah. I suppose I should thank you and Miss Addison. You took care of Eve for me. After all, she had her own part to play in my… accident. Besides, one should never apologize for his actions. Especially when it's for the betterment of the world, right?"

"Is that what you do? Try to better the world?"

"Of course," Machine replied, as if his intention were a foregone conclusion. "The colonies have provided refuge and resources for a dying world. Where's the crime in that?"

"There isn't one. Unless you're selling it to the highest bidder."

Machine laughed, a high-pitched, almost maniacal laughter. Cage bristled at the sound. There was little left of the clever villain he'd known. This man was broken and weak. And out of his mind.

"If you're good at something, you should never do it for free, Macijah. And what's the price of a life, anyway? My colonies will save millions, if not billions of lives. You and I both know that the end is near down here on Earth. The Others gain a stronger foothold every day. The vampire covens have infiltrated almost every level of every government on Earth, gaining followers and slaves through creative pharmaceuticals and our own stupid vanity. Where will we go to escape? And setting aside the artificial ecosystems, our exploration of the Martian colonies has turned up resources that solve a number of problems. Still, you whine about breaking a few eggs."

The boy came back with a tray loaded down with tea service. He had a supernatural grace as he set down the *accoutrements* on the tiny table that seemed to sway with the weight of it. As he straightened, Cage noticed for the first time that the kid had a port in the back of his neck identical to Phoe's.

"I can't say that I'm surprised."

"About?"

Cage nodded toward the kid. "Your own neo-geisha."

Machine chuckled and began scooping sugar cubes into his cup. "Look at me, Macijah. Surely you won't begrudge me a little help." He picked up the cup and offered it to Cage. "Here, have some tea."

"I'm not drinking anything that you offer, Machine."

"Now, Macijah," Machine started. "As you pointed out before, if I'd wanted to kill you, I could have already done that. While I am painfully aware of our... troubled relationship, I brought you here tonight to ask for your help." He sipped from the teacup, slurping and lapping at the tea. He was getting more of it on his shirt than in his mouth. The kid stepped forward and tipped the cup into his mouth, let him drink, and then dabbed at his collar with a handkerchief.

"My help?"

"I know. As strange as it seems, it is even more so to me. But I realize now that all of my demons are coming home to roost." Machine took out the flask again and poured some of the dark liquid inside into his tea. "And don't think that my decision comes lightly, Macijah. Until recent threats, I'd rather be picked at by those hungry werewolves again than ask for your help. But here we are."

"Why in hell would I help you, Machine? If you were on fire, I'd be hard pressed to piss on you."

"Aren't you even the slightest bit interested in my proposal?"

"No."

Machine grinned, and it was horrible. It was almost sad to think of his old adversary in comparison with the shell that sat here in front of him, pieced together and burned. "Come on, Macijah. We have a long history together. It wasn't all bad, was it? We've shared things."

"What have I ever shared with you?"

"How soon you forget dear Eve."

"Eve was never mine to share."

"Really? She was quite… descriptive about you."

"Dear God."

"Oh, don't worry. She was quite complimentary."

Cage's belly lurched. He'd left Death's Door without eating and the thirst was starting to become unbearable. "What do you want, Machine? And make it quick. I'm coming to the end of my patience with this whole thing. You know I wouldn't have a difficult time cutting your heart out with one of those teaspoons. And as you mentioned before, I wouldn't have an ounce of remorse about it."

"Take it easy, old friend." Machine took another sip of his tea, then leaned forward to set the cup and saucer on the table. Cage could hear the slight tremble, but he didn't think the fear was for him.

"What's going on?"

Machine took a deep breath. "How well do you know Maurice Wilder?"

"What do you mean?"

"How much do you know about Maurice's career with MI Six?"

"He was a forensic accountant. A desk jockey that was cozied up with the right people."

Machine laughed that grinding, crackling laugh again. "For a brutal killer, your naiveté is truly surprising."

"I'm not a killer."

"You forget how well I know you. From back to your days with MI Six, long before you had your little accident. You were the best assassin they had."

"That was a long time ago."

"Ah yes, well… it seems we all have a past we'd like to forget. Including your boss. Unfortunately, the past is like a stone tablet—once written, it can never be erased. Someone will always remember."

Cage held Machine's gaze. His good eye was glassy and wet with some unpleasant memory. If he'd touched him, Cage was certain that he would learn a great deal about the withered heart of Derek Machine. Machine knew it too, because he moved away and crossed his arms protectively.

"You and I are so alike, Macijah. I realize that you don't believe that, but it's true. Both of us trying to outrun our past. Holding it close and keeping it secret. But I fear that this time, it's too close. It's coming for me and this time it means to kill me."

"You're not making any sense, Machine."

Machine struggled to his feet. The kid started toward him, but Machine raised a hand to leave him be. He crossed the room to an old desk in the corner. He rummaged inside and pulled out a large envelope. He hobbled back to the table and held it out to Cage. "Take this."

Cage opened the envelope and pulled out a yellowed folder full of moth-eaten papers. "What's this?"

"A dossier. I know it's a bit old school, but such was MI Six. Open it."

Cage flipped through the pages until he came to a photograph. Five people were posed together, smiling into the camera. He recognized one of them as Maurice Wilder and another as Derek Machine. Scrawled across the bottom in marker was "Janus Project."

"You worked for MI Six?"

Machine nodded. "For a time. Unofficially, of course. Myself, Maurice, and three others. Damian Lasko, whom I believe you've met, Oded Nazari, and Natalya Kristokoff. Forever ago, it seems. We were a hunting pack, sent to investigate the covens. The first official mission to do so."

"How can that be?" Cage asked. "The first of the Others were documented in the mid-twentieth century, but the stories go back at least a thousand years."

"Let's say that the government didn't decide to take an interest until then."

"The vampire covens started to cut into their incomes, you mean."

Maurice smiled. "You're so jaded, St. John. For such a dedicated agent, you've quite a contemptuous tone for your masters."

"I have no illusions that should I outlive my usefulness, the IU will have no trouble burning my entire life down."

"Wise," Machine noted. "Of course, they've managed to pump you with enough of their science experiment to keep you going for many years to come."

Cage looked away. The uncertainty of his lifespan was something he didn't like to think about. The vampiric DNA that was the primary component of Ollie's serum gave Cage all of the strengths and weaknesses of the vampire, but he wasn't sure where the immortality fell. Would he live forever while Phoe wasted away, her body failing with age, or would the serum eventually be too much for his cells to contain? Would he simply drop dead or burst into flame? Could he be killed by a stake through the heart? And then there was the child that Phoe carried. Would the child be normal? Would he possess the powers of his parents? Or maybe Phoe's body would eventually reject the alien DNA and cause her to miscarry.

"I can assure you that I have a retirement plan, Machine."

Machine leaned forward with a groan and poured himself another cup of tea. He slurped at it and Cage could hear the burbling inside as he swallowed. It made Cage's stomach roll over. "The five of us were supposed to get close to the higher-ups in the organization, to observe, but not interfere. We were trained and cosmetically altered so as to blend in seamlessly. It worked like a charm and within weeks all of us had been accepted into the Kings' courts. We got in deep, too deep. So much that some of us forgot who we were."

"Maybe some of you were grubby little parasites all along," Cage growled, glaring at Machine.

"Touché," Machine replied. "Say what you like, but even you could be seduced by their decadence. To live as a favored servant of the Quorti is to exist in a hedonistic dream. Youth, beauty, fearlessness... more power than you could possibly imagine."

"Funny, it's never seemed like a dream to me." His stomach growled as if to provide commentary.

"You resist, as I did. We know that no matter what sort of pretty package they wrap it in, being a vampire is to be controlled. From within and without. The thirst consumes your every waking thought, dampening all other desire. The covens are massive hives with the Quorti on top and everyone else biting and clawing and devouring each other to get more power." Machine stared past Cage, his mechanical eye darting back and forth. "Perhaps we're both fools."

"You weren't tempted?"

"Of course I was tempted," Machine spat. "Perhaps if things hadn't gone so wrong, I would have succumbed."

"I'll bite. What happened?"

"There was a gathering in Tokyo. Vampires from every corner of the Earth were there, including the Quorti. They were ready to begin what they called Phase One of their takeover. The Bleeding."

"The Bleeding?"

Machine nodded. "Dramatic, I'll admit. They intended a complete infiltration of vampires into our world. They sought to create vampire-human hybrids, a mix of the races that would be stronger, faster... more intelligent."

"Super humans."

Machine nodded. "Sounds a bit familiar, doesn't it?"

Cage didn't respond. He could taste the bile rising in the back of his throat and if he spoke, he was certain that he would vomit all over Machine. "These hybrids would be their soldiers, but completely subservient to the pureblooded vampires."

"How did they plan to carry out such a thing?"

Machine grinned, looking down as if searching for the answers in the patterns that snaked across the moth-eaten rug. "I think you know the answer to that already."

Cage narrowed his eyes, thinking on Machine's words. Suddenly, it dawned on him. "The amulet."

Machine nodded. "The amulet was the key to the Sin'khari city. I believe Miss Jessica Addison already figured that one out. We found out that the Quorti was in possession of it. They intended to use it to awaken a new species that could infect whole cities in a matter of days."

"What did you do?"

"We didn't have the chance to do much of anything. I was called to a meeting and when I showed up, the other four members of our team were there. I thought it was a bit strange that we had been brought together. After all, we'd been careful to go in from different cities, under different backstories. As far as the vampire community knew, there was no connection between us."

"But someone knew."

"Apparently. Someone had betrayed us. We walked right into a trap that night. There we were, surrounded by drones. Chaos ensued, and we had to fight our way out. I managed to escape with the amulet." He gave a bitter chuckle. "You know we managed to keep that thing hidden for years before Miss Addison found it. Anyway, I barely got out with my life. I assumed that the others were killed until our little incident in New London. That's when I learned of Maurice's ascension to the head of BEAST."

"You left your comrades behind to die?" Cage asked, breathless with disbelief. Cage might be brusque and reckless, but he was loyal to a fault.

"I'm not asking you to understand—"

"You're a coward."

"I'm a realist," Machine snapped, banging his cane on the floor. "If I'd stayed, I'd have been devoured, or worse. Our cover was blown. The covens would have tracked us back to MI Six. More people would have died."

Cage sighed. "So, let me guess. After the smoke cleared, you were nowhere to be found."

"Someone betrayed us. I didn't know who to trust. So, I laid low for a while. MI Six slapped a bandage on the vampire problem by doing what they always do—denying that there is a problem. Including denial of our mission—of our existence."

Cage yawned. "I'm assuming that you're going to eventually land this baby and tell me what I'm doing here. You said you needed my help."

For a long time, Machine was silent. It seemed like he was searching for words. Several times he started to speak, only to take another long sip of his tea. His hands still shook, but Cage was certain now that he was not afraid of him. He was waiting for something, or someone. Machine had the demeanor of a man who knew that his demons were coming for him.

"Whoever is after Wilder isn't going to stop. Someone else made it out of that massacre. I knew it when I heard that you'd found Lasko."

"How do you know about that?"

"You're not the only one with friends on the inside."

"Wilder told you?"

"Of course not. But I have sources." He paused and set his teacup down again. This time he missed the table altogether and the cup crashed to the floor. "Lasko's body... only his skin was left behind?"

"Yes. What does that have to do with anything?"

"I'm not sure. But Lasko is dead, and Wilder came close to dying. Who do you think will be next? It was a secret mission, Macijah. No one knew, but now all of us are under attack. It can't be a coincidence." Machine struggled to his feet. The boy rushed to him, trying to help, but Machine waved him off. "Take the dossier, Macijah. Read it. Draw your own conclusions. I can only pray that you'll find the answer before whoever this is gets to me."

Cage looked down at the folder, leafing through the pages. "Why should I help you? Maybe after all this time you'll finally get what you deserve."

That rattling laughter echoed in the room as Machine limped toward the stairs. "Perhaps both of us will."

Eleven

Phoe was fantasizing about smashing wedding cake into the smiling face of the impossibly thin model on the cover of her bridal magazine. As she clicked through the pages, she was painfully aware of their attractiveness. She laid her hand over her belly that was beginning to swell to a noticeable rounded bump. Her body had become something of a stranger these last couple of months. Though Cage assured her that she was as exceptionally beautiful as she'd always been, when she saw the beginnings of stretch marks at her hips, she had her doubts.

"Dishes done," Cage announced, tossing a towel into the basket by the closet.

"That's great, babe. Thank you. I know it was my night, but I couldn't face it."

"No worries." Cage was graceful as he pulled his shirt over his head and fell into the bed beside her. "Besides, the doctor told you to rest more."

"The doctor is entirely too cautious." She tried not to be annoyed. She knew they were all trying to help, but this mother-hen routine was driving her insane. Ollie had put a bug in Maurice's ear about her delicate condition, so he'd insisted on finding a doctor that was friendly to the IU to check up on her. The doctor had suggested that Phoe not be allowed to shift until after the baby came, which meant that Cage would be relegated to a desk from now on. "I may as well go back to St. Francisville and lie there on the sofa like an old hog waiting for slaughter."

"Don't be so dramatic. He wants to protect you and the baby from Ollie's science experiment."

"Yeah, well my mental health might not hold out much longer. If I have to type in one more case log, I might well lose what's left of my mind."

Cage leaned in and kissed the end of her nose. "It isn't forever, love."

"Holo channel four seventeen," he called. Immediately a holovid projected at the end of the bed. He settled in and she snuggled against his side. He was so warm and always smelled so good. Despite her ill temper, he comforted her. Cage was home. Their lives were so hectic, but he provided a circle of security that she'd been looking for most of her life. But would that be enough once the baby was here? Were they kidding themselves to think that they could provide a safe environment in such a tumultuous world?

And then there was the terrifying realization that she was going to be someone's parent. Her. Mousy Phoebe Addison. Right now her problems were trite, but soon, they wouldn't be her problems. They would be *their* problems. Her and the baby. Cage would be there too, of course, but the baby would be dependent on Phoe for everything.

She had this feeling that her life was no longer her own, and that scared her to death. Would she be able to take care of him? How would she know when he was sick? How would she know how much to feed him or when to put him to bed? Ben was different. When he was home, he was pretty self-sufficient. If they forgot to feed him, he protested. If he was hurt, he shouted. But this was going to be a helpless baby. What if they did something to make him sick?

A particularly loud commercial began to blare, drawing Phoe's attention. Yet another svelte, blonde model danced across the image. "There really should be a law against people looking like that when I'm sitting here looking like this."

"Mmm…" Cage hummed, staring down at his eSlate.

"I mean, look at her. She's probably got more cybernetics and nanobots than any of those sex-bots on Sugoi."

"Probably."

"It isn't fair for those of us who look like beached whales. I mean, every day there's some new and horrifying change to my body, but Miss Healthy Hydro-Meal is shakin' what the good lord gave her all over my holoscreen."

"Uh-huh."

"Cage, are you listening to me?" She punched him playfully on the arm until he finally looked up. "Did you hear anything I said?"

His expression said complete oblivion. "What?"

Cage was the smartest person she'd ever known, but his expression was so blank that she couldn't help giggling. He'd clearly been someplace else for the entirety of their "conversation," such as it was.

"What's so funny?"

"You are," she explained, sitting up. She stared at him another moment, pulling her hair into a messy bun at the top of her head. "All right, then," she started. "Spill it."

"Spill what?"

"What's going on? I've been talking to you for the last ten minutes and you're responding in grunts and huffs like a flatulent old lap dog."

"I beg your pardon?"

"What's the matter with you? Evidently, there's something on your mind."

Cage sighed and got up from the bed. He pushed his hands through his hair in that nervous way he had when he didn't want to reveal something. "It's nothing."

"Liar. You've been either ridiculously sweet—unlike you—or completely oblivious, also unlike you. So go ahead and tell me what's wrong so I can get hysterical and get over it. It will save us so much time."

Cage took a deep breath and crossed his arms over his chest. She could tell that he was trying to decide how much of the truth to tell. He started to speak and then thought better of it. Twice more he tried and failed until finally he blurted, "Machine is alive."

At first Phoe had no idea who or what he was talking about. He was speaking, but the words made no sense. Then it dawned on her. "Derek Machine?"

Cage nodded. "I didn't want to tell you. I thought you'd be worried, and God knows you don't need any more stress right now."

"It's impossible." She rolled out of bed, pulled a robe around herself and wrapped it tight. She was shivering, but it wasn't from the cold. "I thought he'd scuttled off into obscurity with the rest of the sewer rats."

"You know guys like Machine always manage to turn up like dirty knickers."

"Where did you see him?" She couldn't keep the tremble from her voice. Machine was bad news, and she couldn't help thinking that his slinking around Cage after she found out she was pregnant, and the attempt on Maurice's life, was no accident. Whatever his game was, it couldn't be good.

"The night I went to Death's Door. A babydoll approached me. I had planned to negotiate a bit of a top-up, but I noticed he was packing a syringe full of sedative. Naturally I assumed that he was who had been following you, so I forced him into the street. I started to question him, but this werebeast came up behind us and got the drop."

Cage related the story of his impromptu meeting with Machine. The longer he talked, the more apprehensive she became. Machine working for MI6? Wilder working with him? Their connection to Damian Lasko. None of it made any sense. There was a piece missing, and somehow, she and Cage were going to have find it.

"The way I see it, if we find out who betrayed Machine and the others all those years ago, we'll have a good chance of finding our killer."

"We? What's this we business?"

"*We,* meaning me and you. We are partners, after all."

"Yes, but you're in no condition to be chasing a killer."

"What's that supposed to mean?" She stomped her foot. Was he really getting ready to play the *man* card?

"It means that while I'm not doubting your abilities, we have to consider the baby."

Phoe rolled her eyes and heaved a sigh. "Good God, Cage. I'm only a few months along. I'm perfectly capable of doing my job."

"I didn't say you weren't capable, but I can't believe that you would even consider putting the baby at risk."

"At risk of what?"

"Perhaps you're having trouble remembering all those times we've been shot at, attacked, physically altered. Need I go on?"

"And neither of us were hurt. We always come through okay."

"Because we always have before doesn't necessarily mean we will again. Every time we go on a mission, we're risking our lives.

That's lesson one in spy school. And you remember what the doc said—and Ollie. You really shouldn't shift if you don't have to."

"That's ridiculous," she countered.

"No, it isn't. When you burn up as the phoenix and are reborn, your molecules are putting themselves back together. Who's to say that the next time, they won't be able to find their way again?"

"It was fine before," she said through gritted teeth. "You know, all my life people have been telling me I couldn't do this or that because I was a girl. Or because they didn't think I was up to it. Or because I was so sheltered. You're the one that brought me out from under that mantle, so why in hell are you trying to lay it on me again?"

"Because I'm afraid for you," he roared. "I'm not going to lose another family. Not when I can save you. I was too late for Corinne and Lily. I didn't protect them, but I'll be damned if I won't protect you."

"You can't keep us locked in a tower." She turned away, staring out the window at the prowlers and cars rushing by below them. She didn't want to hurt him, but she knew she had. "Look, I know you're afraid. I am too, but Maurice is our friend. And whoever this assassin is, he's killing agents. Who's to say that we won't be next on his hit list?"

She went to where Cage had sat on the bed and embraced him, cradling his head against her belly. She could feel the cold sweat on the back of his neck. He was afraid, not of this hidden assassin, but of losing this life they'd built together. "Come on. Let me help you catch this guy."

For several seconds, he didn't speak. She could almost hear the cogs and gears in his head grinding together as he tried to come up with something. Any excuse to keep her out of the case. Finally, he stared up at her. His eyes were narrow, and his jaw was set, unmoving and stoic. "All right. Do what you want. But no shifting, and if the shit hits the proverbial fan, then you get out. No desperate feats of heroism. No taking a bullet for anyone. If we get in the weeds, you run. Got it?"

"You're giving me conditions under which you'll let me help you?" she snickered.

"Definitely."

"Fine. I accept."

She leaned over and kissed his mouth. A gentle parting of his lips, and she flickered her tongue against the crease, tasting him. His arms wound around her waist, pulling her into him. He rocked back and with a graceful move, swept her into the bed beside him.

Phoe's eyes fluttered as Cage's lips feathered along her throat. His breath was warm and smelled of the glass of wine he'd had with dinner. Her heart pounded in her chest and she could feel the blood rushing in her veins. Since becoming pregnant, she had noticed that all of her senses were heightened. She could see and smell and feel with vivid clarity. At first, the sensation had been disturbing, almost sickening. But now it only made her want more.

Their kiss deepened and she pressed her body against his. She could feel the knot of his arousal growing at her center. Her breath shuddered, and she rocked her pelvis against his. The movement created a friction that drew a groan from deep in his chest. The sound was music to her ears and she could feel a pool of heat collecting between her thighs.

"You seem quite eager tonight, love," he growled before pulling her lower lip between his teeth.

"Well you know what they say…" she whispered. "I'm eating for two." She curled her leg around his, using his body for leverage and rolling him over on his back. She climbed on top of him and began pulling his t-shirt over his head. Cage laughed as she got his arms and head caught in the shirt. She tugged once more, and the shirt came free. She tossed it across the room and immediately went to work on his pants. They were loose with an old-fashioned drawstring at the waist. It didn't take much to slide her hand beneath and free his cock.

"Damn, Phoe…" he gasped as she squeezed him gently. "I have the feeling you're going to be a handful tonight."

She licked her lips and gave a suggestive wink as she let the robe fall from around her shoulders. The camisole she wore left nothing to the imagination and her nipples stood out proudly. Cage ran his hands over the gentle swell of her belly and up to her breasts. He played with the hardened points through the thin fabric, flicking the pads of his fingertips over them and then giving a light pinch.

"You're such a tease," she whispered.

"You're one to talk."

She grinned and sat up on her knees. She started to pull off the camisole, but then felt self-conscious again. Cage must have sensed it and took her hand, guiding it back to the tail of the shirt.

"I want to see you," he whispered. He slipped his hands under the cami and worked it higher. She was clumsy as she pulled it the rest of the way off and stumbled and bounced around until she could pull off the shorts. She crawled forward a little on her hands and knees, throwing her clothes to the floor by the bed.

"Such a view," Cage murmured from behind her. Then she felt his fingertips sliding over the curve of her bottom. His hands cupped the soft globes, then slid lower to caress the backs of her thighs where they came together. There was a gentle pressure as he massaged the soft spot that led from her sex to the forbidden little opening behind. It was such a strange sensation, but she couldn't help arching her back into the caress.

Cage lay back and guided Phoe to straddle him. Her back was to him, but she liked it, not being able to see what he was going to do next. It was thrilling, like she was blindfolded. His cock twitched insistently beneath her. A slight shift and he entered her body. Slowly, she relaxed, taking more of him into her with each breath until finally he was buried inside.

She didn't want to move at first. She'd never felt him so deeply and her sex squeezed and contracted around him, creating a trilling vibration. She let out a long, guttural moan. "Oh my God, Cage…" she groaned.

Cage sat up, cradling her body against his chest. He guided her hips in slow undulations. She laid her head back against his shoulder, riding the thrust of his hips like a gentle wave. When they climaxed, it was a slow build that seemed to go on and on until each tumbled over the edge in turn.

When their breathing started to return to normal, Phoe lay nestled in the crook of Cage's arm. He stroked her hair, brushing his fingertips through the long strands. She could feel herself drifting off with the soft rhythm of his hands.

Her body was relaxed, but her mind was racing.

Derek Machine was asking for their help. Phoe didn't trust him. He'd have killed them both given half a chance, so why was he now so keen to work with them? Then, there was the matter of her mysterious stalker. Cage said when he confronted Machine about it, that he'd been oblivious. So, if not Machine, then who could be following her? And finally, the question remained of who had betrayed the team all those years ago.

Cage's long snore startled her. She turned her head to see that he had fallen asleep, his breath falling lightly in her hair. She traced her fingers along his arm and brushed a stray curl from over his brow. She smiled and pressed her lips against his cheek.

There was only one thing to do. Tomorrow, she was going to see Maurice and get to the bottom of this.

Twelve

Phoe glanced at the clock on the wall for the fifth time in the last three minutes. It seemed as if she'd been waiting outside of Maurice's office forever. She supposed she was a little miffed that she had to wait in the first place. After all, weren't she and Cage the agency's top agents? She cleared her throat and Wilder's secretary, Renee, looked up. She offered a benign smile and went back to typing furiously at the keyboard in front of her. Her nails tapped at the glass panel and Phoe couldn't help wondering how she managed to type and keep those manicured claws.

"Maurice will be with you soon," she called to Phoe.

Phoe smiled back and nodded. "No worries." Funny, she got the distinct impression that Maurice was avoiding her. On a normal day, she would have completely bypassed the secretary and strolled into the office. Today, however, Renee had met her at the door under the guise of getting a cup of coffee and said that Maurice was in with someone and she should wait. However, in the half hour she'd been sitting there, Phoe hadn't seen a soul go in or out of Maurice's office, nor had she heard a word from behind the door.

She glanced at the clock again. Barely a minute had passed. Phoe was starting to get nervous. Cage would be mad as a wet hen if he found out she was here. She'd told him that the doctor had set her a nutritionist appointment this morning, knowing that he had agreed to go with Stefan to question some of Lasko's business associates. She wanted to talk to Wilder alone. She thought that maybe she could get him to open up to her.

Finally, the door opened. Maurice wandered out, straightening his tie. Phoe was not surprised to see that he was all alone. However, Maurice looked surprised as hell to see her. Almost afraid. She stood up and put on her friendliest nonchalant smile. "Finally, Maurice. Were you taking a shower in there? Entertaining?"

"Oh, hi. Phoe. I wasn't expecting to see you this morning."

Phoe threw a pointed glare Renee's way. "Oh yeah? I've been waiting out here for about a half hour."

"Ah… well. I was on an important phone call. I'm sorry I kept you waiting."

She wanted to call him and Renee on the bullshit, but Phoe figured it best to get to the heart of the matter. "I needed to talk to you. Without Cage."

Maurice looked uncomfortable. He was avoiding looking her in the eye. He shifted

from foot to foot. "Actually, Phoe… I have an appointment. I can't talk right now, but maybe you could come back later?"

"No, I can't come back later. I need to talk to you now."

Maurice looked from Phoe to Renee. His eyes darted everywhere. Phoe could tell that he was trying to think of a good excuse to blow her off, but she wasn't going to budge. He had the answers she was looking for. When he'd decided she wasn't going to leave without some kind of satisfaction, he sighed. "Fine. Come on in. I guess I can spare a few minutes." Maurice stepped aside and waved her to cross into his office.

When they stepped inside, Phoe nearly gasped at what she saw. Every other time she'd been here, the place was immaculate. Everything in its place, a clear desktop, not a speck of dust in sight. This morning, papers were strewn over the desk in haphazard piles. Old storage boxes with their tops off littered the floor, and now that she took a closer look, Maurice seemed disheveled in a way she'd never seen him before.

"Thank you," Phoe said, throwing her purse and coat down on a chair that had books stacked on it.

"Of course," Maurice replied. "You're one of my top agents. I always have time for you."

Out of the corner of her eye, Phoe was able to identify several old paper files stacked on his desk. "I appreciate that, Maurice."

"Can I get you anything? Coffee? Tea?"

Phoe shook her head. "Sadly, no. My doctor is insisting I lay off that stuff."

"Doctors tend to be such worrywarts," Maurice commiserated. "So, what brings you to see me on such short notice?"

"I didn't realize I had to make an appointment."

Maurice chuckled nervously. "Oh… no, of course not, but uh… I would have made some accommodations to my schedule had I known. You see, I have a meeting with the Secretary of Interplanetary Governance this morning."

"That sounds important."

"Indeed," Maurice said. "Must keep the powers that be happy, you know."

Phoe nodded. "Well I won't take up much of your time, Maurice. I have a couple of questions."

"Such as?"

"Such as why you've been thwarting any attempt whatsoever to find the guy who tried to kill you."

"Phoebe… I've already told you…"

"Yes, several times, and you haven't told us the truth yet."

Maurice groaned in exasperation, pushing back from his desk to stand. "It's been three months. The bullet barely grazed me."

"Barely grazed you? The doctor in St. Francisville said that another millimeter to the left and we'd have been planning your funeral instead of a wedding."

"I've been shot worse, Phoebe."

"Not in my front yard. By someone whose skin was found in a skeevy motel a few hours later."

Maurice avoided eye contact and began to pace. "I don't understand why you and Cage can't let this go."

"Because it's pretty fucking obvious that you know more about this than you're letting on. And because I've got a lot on my plate right now and my partner can't seem to help me with it because he's obsessing about finding this killer before he tries again."

He stopped pacing long enough to say, "I don't know what to tell you, Phoebe."

"You can start with this." She opened her bag and pulled out Machine's file on the vampire operation. She pushed it across the desk toward Maurice. He stared down at the file as if it were a dangerous insect. He started to open it but pulled his hand back before it touched.

"Where did you get this?"

"Never mind that. The hazard of only knowing spies."

"Does Cage know you have this?"

"Cage doesn't even know I'm here."

"It was a long time ago, Phoe."

"Evidently not so long for someone."

Maurice sat behind his desk then stood up and resumed pacing. His fingertips were poised against his mouth as if he were searching for the words to explain himself. He was considering which lie to tell her. Another hazard of knowing spies: most of them never told the truth. "What do you need to know that this file hasn't already told you? I was on a mission with MI Six. Things went south. I barely got out with my life. What else is there to say?"

"Plenty. Somebody who was involved wants you dead. I need to know why."

"There's no reason to believe that the attempt on my life has anything to do with this. Over the course of my terribly long career, I've made my fair share of enemies. If you don't believe me, ask Cage. Death threats are an occupational hazard. You should get used to it."

Phoe couldn't help laughing. "Cage was right. You're a shit spy, Maurice."

"I beg your pardon?"

"You're a terrible liar. Did you think I didn't read that file? You and Lasko were both on that team. He's dead and you came damn close."

"We're both former MI Six. That's barely a connection."

"And I got this file from Derek Machine. Also, a member of the team. He's scared shitless because he's thinks he's the next on this assassin's list."

Maurice looked like a fish out of water, desperate to breathe. It was almost comical. "Derek Machine? You ought not be keeping company with a man like him."

"A dangerous man?"

"A liar. Derek Machine was a member of MI Six, yes, but he was tossed out in disgrace."

"How so?"

"How much did he tell you about our last mission together?"

"Everything," Phoe lied.

Maurice shook his head. "I don't think so. If he did, you wouldn't be here."

Phoe glared. Her mind raced trying to think of something to say that wouldn't overplay her hand. If she said too much, Maurice was going to clam up. The art of interrogating someone without trying to seem like you're interrogating them—it was a form of subtlety that she had not yet grasped. "He told Cage that you were in deep with the covens. That someone betrayed you, completely blowing the mission and nearly getting all of you killed."

"And you want to know who betrayed us."

"It would be a start."

Maurice smiled. "Is the answer really so hard to find, Phoebe?"

"What do you mean?"

"You got your information from Derek Machine, yes?"

"I told you that."

"But did you consider that perhaps he was telling you and Cage everything in order to hide his own guilt?"

"What do you mean?"

"The vampires had something that Machine wanted above all things."

"What's that?"

Maurice picked up the dossier and flipped through it. In the back was what looked like an impossibly thin piece of glass. He set it on the table in front of Phoe and a series of photographs appeared in the air above. He flipped through several of them, obviously looking for something. Phoe recognized one of the images as the Quorti of the vampire covens, Ankhil, and a shiver rolled down her spine. The next snap was a shot of the team together. Phoe recognized younger Maurice and Derek. With a swipe of his fingers, Maurice drew the image closer and zoomed in on Machine. "Can you see it?"

Phoe stared at the image, looking for anything strange. Then she saw it. A glimmer peeking from under Machine's shirt. As Wilder moved in closer on the picture, sharpening the image, recognition flooded in. The medallion Jess had sent her in St. Francisville, the catalyst that had set her on this path, was tied around his throat. "The key."

"Exactly," Maurice said. "The medallion. The same one that he nearly killed you for. When MI Six sent us to investigate the covens, they had no idea how widespread they already were. They used their ability to blend into our world much more efficiently than we had ever expected. Machine started to see the possibilities in joining them. He grew closer than the rest of us to the Quorti, who was grooming Machine to be his general. Giving him possession of that medallion was a symbol of his station in the hierarchy. Machine sold all of us out to keep it."

"Why? What use would it have been to him?"

"Do you realize what that medallion is?"

Phoe shrugged. "Only the stories. The door to some hidden city, right?"

Maurice laughed, bitter and cool. "It's so much more than that. 'Hidden city' implies that the medallion is merely some archaeological find. But that medallion is power absolute. Whomever controls the doorway controls the fate of our world. Surely you must understand this."

"Which is why he wanted it back from Jess."

Maurice nodded. "But he was a fool. Machine has no respect for anyone or anything. All he cares about is money. He sought to use the medallion to bring about some kind of tourist apocalypse."

"How? I wouldn't think that the vampires would give away something so valuable. Assuming it's as important as you say it is."

"They never intended to give it to him. Not really. They would let him keep possession of it, recognizing it that his place with MI Six could be of use. But they never let him forget that he was still a servant of the Quorti. Perhaps they underestimated how cunning he could be. All I know is that the night we were exposed to the Quorti, Ankhil ordered our execution. He should have let his drones kill us right there, but the vampires can't resist a bit of theatre. They intended to drain us slowly in a Sin'khari ritual. We knew we had to get away. The Quorti is cruel and unforgiving. They would have tapped our veins like a maple tree and poured our blood like wine. Excruciating torture."

"But you still didn't know who the turncoat was."

Maurice shook his head. Phoe could see that the memories were painful. Cage had always complained that Wilder was a terrible field agent who would prefer to sit behind a desk, never getting his hands dirty. Perhaps he wasn't lazy, but afraid. Phoe shuddered, remembering her own brush with the vampires and how close she'd come to suffering the same fate.

"We were separated and thrown into cells. Lasko and I were locked up together, Nazari and Kristokoff were paired, and we assumed that Machine was on his own. We managed to get past our guards to the chamber where the Quorti was waiting. We thought that maybe if we could kill him, we could stop it. When we made it into the chamber, everything went to hell. There were so many of them. Blood and smoke and... I kept shooting, and I managed to escape with my life. I thought the others were dead, and then when Machine turned up with the medallion on New London, I knew then that he'd been the one who sold us out to the Quorti."

"Did you try to confront him?"

"Why bother? When his house blew up on New London, I assumed, as we all did, that he'd been killed. We had the medallion back and all was right with the world."

"Until now."

Maurice nodded and stood in front of her. "And now, I really must go, Phoe." He buttoned his suit jacket and looked at the clock.

"Of course," Phoe said. Her head was starting to spin. Maurice's story was definitive, but she could tell that he was holding something back. In the last few years, she'd learned to tell when someone, especially an agent, was lying. Maurice was most definitely not telling her the truth.

The question was: why?

Thirteen

Phoe felt more than dissatisfied as she exited through the glass doors at the IU building and started toward the Tube station. She went over Maurice's explanation, trying to match it up with what Cage had shared about Machine's story. Somebody was hiding something, but she couldn't quite put her finger on who. Before she had much time to think about it, her eSlate buzzed against her side. She flipped it over in her hand to see Cage's name glowing bright on the screen.

"Hey babe," she said, trying to sound casual.

"Where have you been? I've been trying to call you for at least an hour."

She tried to think fast. Should she tell him where she's been? Would it upset him to know that she'd taken it upon herself to confront Maurice with Machine's story? "Uh… well… I've been to HQ."

"What were you doing over there?"

"Talking to Maurice about some things. Where are you?"

"I'm at the Maglev. I need you to meet me."

"The Maglev? What on earth are you doing there?"

"Waiting for you." Cage grinned. "Get a cab and come on."

"Romantic getaway?"

"Depends greatly upon your definition of romance."

Phoe giggled. She could almost see his eyebrows arched in that sly way he had that looked both teasing and ominous. "I'm almost afraid to ask."

She managed to hail a cab even though the street was crowded with commuters. Apparently being pregnant had some advantages. She clamored into the back of the black cab, wondering if she ought to tell the driver to go by the flat first. Cage always had a way of surprising her with these little rendezvous. It was one of the things she loved about him, but spontaneity had never been her strong suit.

"Where to, Mum?" cabbie asked, his accent a too-perfect cockney brogue. Obviously a 'borg driver.

"Paddington Station," Phoe answered. "Maglev gate."

When interplanetary travel began to become commonplace, the land transportation industry began to boom. Maglev technology had been around for more than a century, but only in the last few decades had it become the most efficient and luxurious way to travel. Gilded light fixtures reminiscent of the gas lamps on Absinthia, marble columns, and sparkling hardwood floors gave the place an Old World extravagance that was in complete opposition of the futuristic mode of travel.

When Phoe arrived at the gate, Cage was standing there waiting, looking like a god in his dark trousers and gray, close-fitting sweater. He didn't appear to be an international man of mystery today, but the hero of some tawdry romance novel. Something was definitely up.

"What took you so long?" he teased, clasping her hand and pulling her into an affectionate embrace. His body was warm and his color high. He'd gone out to feed this morning. That explained a lot.

Phoe didn't ask Cage much about his eating habits. She was kind of afraid to know how he satisfied the bloodthirsty vampire within. True, he hated to be thought of as a vampire—a nasty parasite—but he couldn't escape the fact that he needed blood to survive.

"Traffic was murder."

"I'm not surprised," he said. "But the important thing is, you're here now." He leaned in to kiss her, but she backed away out of his reach. "What?"

"You wanna tell me what's going on?" She was suspicious of his silly, boyish attitude. Cage had a great sense of humor and was always fun to be around, but Phoe wouldn't describe him as giddy or sappily affectionate.

He thought for a moment, obviously considering his words carefully. "What are you on about? Can't I take my fiancée on a trip before our wedding?" He held up the hand that held an overnight bag.

Phoe chuckled and wound her arms around his waist. "I thought that's what the honeymoon was for."

"But by then there'll be three of us. Come on, let's have a little adventure together. Just me and you."

She allowed Cage to lead her onto the Maglev. As they made their way to their seats in the first-class cabin, she was reminded of the first time they met nearly three years ago. She smiled, remembering how timid she had been. The old Phoe had never been more than a hundred miles away from her home. The only adventures she'd had up to that point had ended in tragedy, scaring her back to that rattling old farmhouse in St. Francisville.

"Remember the first time we met? You told me how to get to my seat."

Cage nodded. "You were so cute. I could barely hear you when you said your name. The only reason I knew what you were asking was when you shook your ticket in my face."

"Gee, I dunno why I'd be intimidated by you. You seem to forget that shortly after that conversation, I watched you throw a werewolf through a wall."

Cage laughed. "Oh yeah."

"Please find your seats," an electronic voice droned overhead. "The Bargau Express will be departing in fifteen minutes and arriving in Romania at seventeen hundred hours."

"Romania?" she asked. "We're going to Romania?"

He opened the overhead compartment and shoved their overnight bag inside. "I thought it might be fun to go someplace different."

Phoe nodded. "I agree. But Romania? You've never expressed any interest in Romania." Something about the country stood out in her mind. It was by all accounts, a fabulous place to visit, but there was something more. Something important happened in Romania.

"It's an ancient place. Full of history. I thought we could spend a couple of days wandering around, absorbing the culture."

She smiled and tilted her head as she brushed past him to sit down at the seat by the window. "God, you're a terrible liar for a spy."

"What?"

"You've never absorbed culture in your life. So, spill it, St. John. What the hell are we going to Romania for?"

"Do you think so little of me? That I'm a stupid oaf that you occasionally let fall on top of you?"

"Of course not, but you're acting like a pod person. What's up?"

Cage sighed and sat down beside her deflated. Evidently, Phoe knew him better than he imagined. "The truth is, I do want to take you to Romania for a good time."

"But?"

"But I also have a guy there that I need to see."

Phoe nodded. "A guy?"

"Former secret police. He helped me out after the Splice."

"You trust him?"

"I wouldn't go that far. But, he knows everything about vampires. Reason being—he is one."

Her breath caught in her chest, making her gasp and cough. "Wait. What?"

"He's a vampire. He fell in with the covens years ago. Whatever went down with Wilder, I can almost promise you that Vladimir knows about it."

She gave him a blank stare. Was he honestly suggesting that they get help from a vampire? That was almost as insane as joining forces with Derek Machine. In Cage's own words, vampires were disgusting parasites who would stop at nothing to satisfy their lust for blood and power. They could easily be walking into a trap. "Don't you think this might be a bit…"

"Dangerous? Probably. But Vlad's a good guy. You'll like him. He has a way with women."

"I'm sure."

"And let's not forget that you were the one who was tired of being treated like an invalid."

Her eyes felt as if they would pop out of her head as she stared at him. "I didn't mean that I wanted to take on a vampire coven on our own."

"Oh, we aren't going to be taking them on." He turned and cradled her face between his enormous hands. "I promise. I would never take you into a situation where I couldn't guarantee your safety. Or the safety of our child."

"But…"

He leaned in and kissed her gently. "Trust me."

She did trust him. Cage was the first and only person in her life that she'd ever trusted completely. The only person she had ever been able to depend on. That wasn't to say that she didn't love and trust her own family. She and Jess had become closer in the last three years than they ever had been. But Jessica had always been so caught up in her own life that she never had room for her little sister. Then, there was their mother.

Olivia Addison was, by all outside reports, the perfect mother. She was overbearing with her affection, kind, a nurturer to everyone she knew—and also one of the most passive-aggressive souls ever to walk the earth. Ever since Phoe was a child, her mother had been sickly or depressed, and needed constant attention. When Phoe's father left, Jess was already away at school and it had been up to Phoe to fill in that gap. Then, when it was time for college, her mother got sick and Phoe ended up attending the local university. After her mother died, Phoe realized that she'd spent her entire life taking care of someone else.

But then, she met Cage and her whole life changed. He took care of her. He kept his promises. There was no reason to believe that he wouldn't keep her safe this time.

She snuggled under his arm as the Maglev began to move. As they picked up speed, she watched the city fade and give way to the countryside until everything blurred together. It was starting to make her dizzy and she closed her eyes. Soon, she was falling asleep.

***

"Julian," Cage said loud enough to wake Phoe, who had been asleep the better part of an hour.

She jumped, jarred from her sleep. "What?" she mumbled.

Cage's nerves were getting the better of him. The truth was, he and Vlad had not parted on the best of terms. They were friends, but Vladimir had embraced the vampire lifestyle with fervor—a choice that Cage found abhorrent. Maurice always said that the former secret police were government-sanctioned thugs, not much different than those goons that had assaulted Phoe on their first train ride together.

Cage had been a government-sanctioned thug himself, but running with vampires was a whole other level. Still, Vlad might have the answers they're looking for.

"What are you talking about?"

"I think if this baby is a boy, we should call him Julian."

Phoe wrinkled her nose. "Really? It's kind of a weird name."

Cage shrugged. "Not any stranger than Macijah."

"True. But I thought we were going to do better for our children."

Cage feigned offense, gasping and clutching his chest. "You're absolutely right. *Phoebe*."

"I never said my name wasn't weird." Phoe smiled and clasped Cage's hand between hers. "My only problem with Julian is that he'll forever be known as Jules."

Cage shrugged. "That might not be so bad. Jules Verne was an amazing writer."

"How about Christopher?"

Cage raised an eyebrow. "No."

"What's wrong with it?"

"It sounds so… pedestrian."

"Oh yes, because *Julian* sounds like something that won't get our child thrown in every dumpster in London."

"Jonathan?"

"I think we should knock all of the J names off the list. They'll sound ridiculous with St. John. I mean, Jonathan St. John? Sounds like a weatherman. But you know, the baby might be a girl."

"God, don't say that." Cage coughed. His belly rolled over at the thought. He knew what lurked in the minds of men. "I don't think I could take the stress."

Phoe rolled her eyes and started to answer, but her words were drowned out by the shrieking of the brakes on the Maglev. "Why are we stopping?" she asked. "We're nowhere near Romania."

"*Passengers. We are experiencing some technical difficulties at this time,*" a freakishly pleasant, robotic voice said over the loudspeaker. "*The conductor asks that all passengers exit from one of the doors located at the front or rear of the carriage. We will be up and running again shortly. Thank you for your patience.*"

Phoe groaned as she sat up and stretched. "I had just gotten comfortable."

The passengers in first class began to rise from their seats. A general din of grumbling filled the train as the stewards began herding them out of the doors and into the cool afternoon. It was a dreary day and the place where they had stopped was in the middle of nowhere. Ahead was a vast forest, tightly packed with fiery trees.

Beyond them, Cage could see the jagged mountain range they would have to cross to get to Romania.

"Why in hell are they getting us off the train out here?" Phoe asked, reaching into the overhead compartment to grab her shoulder bag. "They could have at least picked a place more populated."

Cage couldn't help agreeing. Unless it was an egregious emergency, it was highly irregular for the train to stop in such a place—even worse, to make all the passengers get off in the middle of an open field in an area known to be crawling with Others and the usual wildlife. "This thing better be ready to explode."

The crowd of passengers were like sheep as they made their way down the aisle toward the exits. Cage could feel the heat set in beneath his skin as his annoyance level rose. He hated crowds. Even more so when everyone seemed to be ambling slowly in front of him. Phoe gripped his hand tight, knowing that he was close to losing his shit in this tightly enclosed space.

And then the lights went out.

"Oh no." Phoe sighed. As people will do, everyone began to shout and push to get out of the train faster. Evidently, they'd decided that the end times were nigh, and they were all going to die if they didn't get out of the carriage posthaste.

Cage grabbed Phoe's hand. He wasn't sure why, but something about this wasn't right. Maglev transportation was safe and efficient. There was rarely a malfunction. Tiny hairs on the back of his neck stood up and once more he could feel the shift begin to crawl beneath his skin. "We have to get out of here," he said, keeping his voice low.

"Feeling claustrophobic?"

"Something strange is going on."

"What are you talking about?"

The Maglev gave a lurch, spilling several passengers out of the doors, adding to the chaos. That was all it took and suddenly their orderly exit of the train became a mad rush for the doors. Even the electronic announcement started to sound uneasy as the passengers tried to get off.

"I'm not sure," Cage replied.

Screams could be heard from outside, and then the carriage shook again. Something crashed overhead, and Cage could hear what sounded like footsteps banging against the roof of the train.

Another flicker and the lights went out for good. The automatic doors slammed shut, locking in place with the loss of power.

"Oh my God."

"What's happening?"

"What is that?"

"Everyone calm down," Phoe shouted. "I'm sure the power will be back in a second."

In their panic, the crowd behind Cage and Phoe started to push forward. Some tried to get to the door, others tried to pry open the doors and windows. Another scream rang out, and the crowd shifted, pulling Cage and Phoe apart. The carriage shook as more of whatever it was on the roof landed.

"Do you hear that?" Cage asked, pointing upward.

Her eyes widened as she tried desperately to listen over the din of chaos. "What the hell is that?"

Cage tried to focus on the sounds coming from the cabin's roof.

"Maybe they're working on the train?" she asked as another loud bang came from overhead and sparks rained down over their heads. Then the shrieking sound of metal being peeled back made everyone gasp. They held their ears as it screeched, and a creature pulled back the roof of the carriage like a can lid.

"Cage, look out," Phoe screamed as what could only be a vampire dropped down from the gaping hole in the roof.

The force of the explosion rocked the carriage again and Phoe fell backward, dropping Cage's hand. "Phoe," he shouted but the vampire kicked him hard in the belly, sending him sprawling back along the narrow aisle. The vampire hissed and stretched to his full height as he loomed over Cage. Its size was incredible, like no vampire Cage had ever seen. It was humanoid, yet its form was distorted with a freakishly lean body and limbs that seemed stretched. Its back arched strangely and its mouth was too large. This drone didn't appear to be normal. It had obviously been altered in some way.

The crowd was screaming in earnest now as more vampires dropped from the ceiling and tore the doors open to spill inside the carriage. Cage wanted to shift, the urge almost unbearable, but he wasn't sure it wouldn't do more harm than good.

"Cage St. John," the vampire snarled. "We've been lookin' all over for you, mate."

"Looks like you found me," Cage said, getting to his feet. He flashed his eyes. His mouth ached as the fangs broke through the thin membrane, growing with his anger. He took an attack stance and growled at the vampire. It lunged at him, grabbing Cage by throat and raising him off the floor. The talons dug into his throat and Cage could feel the venom burning.

"So I did." The vampire grinned, throwing him down.

Cage fell over a row of seats, the edge of his foot kicking the luggage compartment and spilling bags in a heavy torrent all around him. He started to his feet but stumbled as another bag fell down. His head was cloudy, but he could see that the vampires had completely torn the carriage apart, and more were pouring in with every passing second. But there was something strange. These were not mere killing drones. Some were pulling the passengers aside, biting them, then letting them drop.

"C'mon, mate," the vampire hissed, stalking toward him, kicking bags out of the way and shoving passengers out of the way. "I expected more from you."

"If it's me you want," Cage called, "let's take it outside and away from these people."

"Such a boy scout for someone who used to be so reckless," the vampire said. He raised his head and inhaled, sniffing the air. "Can't you smell them, St. John? Their fear makes their blood smell so sweet."

Cage's mouth watered. He could smell them. The warm, wet, human blood that flowed so freely in their veins. It had been so long since he'd had such a rich indulgence.

"Cage," Phoe's scream cleared his head a little. He looked to her as the floor beneath them started to give way. More vampires began to claw their way through. Phoe was knocked backward into a group of passengers as they burst into the carriage. She recovered quickly and delivered a hard kick to the first vampire that came through. It sputtered and spat, falling back. She punched one then whipped around, drawing her dagger, quick and sure, across the throat of another.

Cage gave a smug grin, but his satisfaction was short-lived. The vampire that loomed over him laughed. "Looks like I went after the wrong agent." It turned and started toward where Phoe was holding her own.

Rage exploded inside Cage as he felt his body growing, pulling his shirt tight across his chest. His spine tingled as it straightened, and his hands became claws. His mouth grew, breaking his jaw and widening to accommodate razor-sharp teeth.

He leapt, grabbing the edges of the shelves, using them for leverage to propel him over the heads of the vampires that were now diving into the crowds of passengers still trying to get out of the death trap they'd created. The vampire, obviously the leader of the operation, grabbed for Phoe, pulling her by the back of the shirt and off another drone that was feeding on an old lady still clutching her purse. Phoe thrashed, trying to get away, but the vampire pulled her up high and slammed her down across the backs of the seats.

Cage heard Phoe cry out as she hit the floor. His vision clouded red and he swung over the crowd and came down on top of the leader. He heard the bones crack in its back as he pressed his full weight against the vampire's spine. It hissed and screamed, trying to make its limbs work. Cage pulled it up, sinking his teeth into the soft spot at the thing's shoulder and neck. The hot, stagnant blood exploded, peppering Cage's cheeks with the black stuff. It tasted sour, but he didn't care. Pulling back, he tore a chunk of the vampire's flesh off with his teeth, then twisted the head until he felt the bones give way.

Cage tossed the body aside and threw himself into the fray. By now, he couldn't tell which were vampires and who were passengers trying to avoid being eaten. The crowd was a seething, screaming mass, piling on top of one another.

The rage of the berserker he'd let come out blinded him as he went after one vampire then another. He didn't have a gun or dagger, but he didn't need one. It was almost exhilarating to tear them apart with his bare hands.

"Cage." Phoe's voice broke through the haze of his frenzy.

He looked up to see most of the vampires gone and only a few straggling passengers stumbling through the holes in the sides of the carriage and out into the night. Only Phoe stood amid a pile of bodies. She was silently pleading with him. She stood at an unnatural angle and then Cage saw that she was being held by one of the drones who nuzzled at Phoe's throat lovingly, licking at the thick vein that pulsed beneath the skin.

"Such a sweet bit of tasty flesh," the vampire crooned. "Her heart races looking at you, St. John. This must be your mate."

"Let her go," Cage hissed. His voice sounded foreign to him, more creature than man.

"Will you give your life for her?" The thing drew one of its claws along Phoe's cheek. A bubble of blood appeared and wept down her face. The drone lapped at it. Phoe winced at the venom as it infected the wound. "Mmm… I see why you like her."

"Cage, go," Phoe whispered. "Don't fall for its tricks."

"Oooh… the plot thickens," the drone said. "Which one of you will make the sacrifice?"

"Either way, you die," Cage growled.

"But will you get to me in time to save her life?" The vampire was a flash of movement, rushing past Cage to the other end of the carriage, then it leapt through the hole in the ceiling, carrying Phoe.

Suddenly, the vampire shrieked and loosened its grip on Phoe, letting her go, and she fell through the hole. Cage was there to catch her before she hit the floor. The pointed tip of Phoe's silver dagger glimmered at the base of the vampire's throat. One of the Maglev stewards appeared behind the vampire, shoving the dagger in to the hilt, then twisting until the blade went up through its skull, nearly splitting it in two before throwing the body aside.

"You're welcome," the steward said, wiping the blade on her neat pencil skirt before tossing it back down to Phoe. "Better get out of there. I can hear the sirens already."

Fourteen

Phoe couldn't help cowering as Cage reached for her. She'd seen him like this once before—on Absinthia, and then, as now, she wondered how far he'd gone and if she could bring him back. But today, she witnessed a brutality she'd never seen him engage in, ferocity she could never have imagined. True, she'd held her own against the onslaught of drones, but he'd been something... other. There were bodies all around, but not only that—limbs that had been torn from the vampires still quivered on the ground, masses of wet flesh that steamed in the cool evening. Pools of blood oozed and coalesced as if seeking out something to hold onto. Phoe's stomach rolled over and she turned away, trying to stave off the coppery stench. She didn't want to consider the fact that some of these people had been innocent passengers.

"It's all right, love," Cage rasped. "It's me. I'm in control."

But was he really? His eyes, usually a cool blue, had turned a fearsome red that echoed the color of the blood that dripped from the corners of his mouth.

"I'm not sure I can do this," she whimpered, nearly swooning.

Cage offered his hand and she paused, considering if it was safe to take it. "It's okay. I'll help you."

She grasped his fingers and let him pull her into a tight embrace. As soon as she felt his heat, relief and reassurance washed over her. His strength and scent was so familiar and she could see the man she loved lurking inside of this monster. He held her tight as he leapt up to the edge of the hole in the ceiling, then climbed out.

The vampires had all but disappeared, save for a few that lay gravely injured. The steward that had saved their lives made short work of them, firing bullets into their brains as she picked her way over the bodies. Groups of passengers huddled together, shuddering with every shot.

"Is that really necessary?" Phoe called when they reached the ground. "You're scaring the passengers."

"Well," the steward began, "we could leave them here to reanimate. They'd track us into those hills and pick us off as the sun went down. Personally, I think the passengers would rather have a little jump scare now than be dinner later."

Phoe gazed out over the vast nothingness in which they found themselves. She could see now that their carriage had become disconnected from the rest of the Maglev. She wondered how long it had been since they were left behind. It was obvious that the rest of the train was long gone.

"Help me, please. The pain of it…"

Phoe looked up to see the steward bending over one of the victims who lay on the ground. His three-piece suit was splattered with the black blood of the drones. His throat had a gash so deep that it appeared his head was hanging by a thread. Phoe's belly flopped once more and she doubled over, hiding her face in the crook of Cage's arm.

"Is he all right?" Cage asked.

The steward didn't answer but placed the butt of her gun between the man's eyes and pulled the trigger. "No."

"Stop it," Phoe screamed, breaking away from Cage and running to the steward. She shoved her to the ground, pulling back her fist to strike.

"Back off, ultra," the steward snarled, pointing the gun at Phoe as she got to her feet. "I won't mind killing you."

Cage was there in a flash, grabbing the steward's gun. He twisted her arm behind her back and pulled her up fast, his fangs poised at her throat. "I haven't let go of the monster quite yet, so please believe that if you displace one hair on her head that you'll be dead before the bullet leaves the chamber."

"Take it easy, vampire." The steward winced as he twisted her arm higher.

"I wouldn't call him that if I were you," Phoe cautioned. "He hates it."

"Noted," the steward said, letting the gun drop.

Cage released the woman and she stumbled away. "But I don't know why you're being so sentimental. I was saving that poor bastard's life."

"By shooting him?"

"He was infected. In case you missed it, that carriage was attacked by vampires. A particularly nasty breed of vampires."

"But that man was innocent," Phoe protested. She took a deep breath and willed herself not to vomit. The smell of death was heavy and thick. She could almost see it rising in the mist like a poisonous fume. "There was no reason to shoot him."

"No, that man was bitten by a drone."

"Exactly," Cage said, searching the drone bodies for weapons. "No reason to think they would turn unless they'd tasted vampire blood."

"Not these drones. As I said they are a particularly nasty breed. These guys aren't so much born as made in a lab."

"To what end?" Phoe asked.

"Isn't it obvious?" The woman sighed heavily, rolling her eyes at Phoe in a way that made her want to knock them down her throat. "To spread their disease. Drop one vampire into a nest of civilians and you can turn the whole lot into ruthless killers. The covens have created a specialized venom that can immediately infect the host."

"Impossible," Cage grumbled. "The IU tried it already. The newborns would be crazed with thirst or insane with the shock. They'd tear themselves apart before they could infiltrate the area."

"Think the good guys are the only ones with scientists?" She chuckled to herself and pulled the shoulder bag off a dead passenger. She began filling it with whatever she could find strewn along the ground.

Phoe didn't like this person. She reminded her entirely too much of Eve Manning. True, she'd saved their lives, but that didn't necessarily mean a thing in this world. "Who are you, anyway?" she asked finally.

"The woman who saved your skins." She squinted at the horizon where the sun was nearly gone. "Come on. It'll be dark soon. The next town is a couple of miles down. Pray we can get a car that can take us the rest of the way to Romania."

"How did you know we were going to Romania?" Cage asked.

"Vladimir Antonescu sent me," she replied. She tossed Phoe an autopistol. "Those hills will be crawling with newborn vamps pretty soon. I trust you can use that thing?"

Phoe opened the magazine, checking the plasma packs before slamming it shut. She flicked the safety off and pointed it at the woman's feet. She fired two rounds, making the woman stumble backward. "I think I can handle it."

Phoe glanced at Cage, who was looking more and more like himself again, hoping that he was going to refuse to go anywhere with this woman. This was all too convenient. First, her weird conversation with Maurice. Then, Cage whisking her off to see this questionable friend of his. The vampire attack, and now this perfect stranger leading them into the wilderness.

She took Cage's offered hand as they fell into step behind the woman. "Are you sure we should be following this person?" she whispered. "We don't know anything about her. She won't even tell us her name."

"Welcome to that most time-honored spy-game practice of 'what choice have we got?'"

"Yeah, but what about the survivors? Shouldn't we stay with them until help arrives? She said this place would be crawling with newborn vampires by nightfall. We can't leave the people behind."

"I'm sure that help is on the way. I can hear the sirens in the distance."

"But what if—"

"Let's go," the woman shouted. She was already a hundred yards ahead of them.

"Look, Vlad sent her to find us," Cage stated.

"Yeah, and that's another thing," Phoe hissed. "I'm not crazy about this Vladimir fellow either. We could be walking straight into a trap."

"I trust him," Cage said. "I'm not suggesting not to be cautious, but Vlad is a good guy. Besides, he owes me a favor."

Phoe wasn't sure her mind was at ease, but she fell into step beside Cage. They walked across an open field, leaving the scant surviving passengers behind. She gazed over her shoulder guiltily. "I hope help gets here soon. The sun's nearly gone."

"They'll be fine," Cage assured her.

"Cage St. John," Phoe started, "what if you'd said that about me the first time we met? You and those goons wrecked the Maglev and you were about to walk away, remember?"

Cage chuckled, sliding his arm around her waist as they walked. "I do. And I remember how you offered to pay me." He scratched his chin. "Now that I think of it, you never did give me the money."

"Oh, darling, I paid with nature's credit card." Phoe gave an exaggerated huff. She had to admit that despite all the problems they'd encountered—and being attacked and nearly dying more times than she cared to remember—adventures with Cage were always fun.

"Cage St. John?" the woman asked, stopping short. She turned and stared at Cage as if he were a circus act. "You're Cage St. John?"

He nodded. "Yes. What of it?"

The woman smiled, shaking her head. "Vlad didn't tell me I was coming to retrieve Macijah St. John. Honestly, I'm kind of disappointed that you needed retrieving."

"What are you talking about?" Phoe asked. She was past annoyed with this bitch. She hated when someone acted like they were part of an inside joke that didn't include her.

"Cage here's a legend… in certain circles."

"What circles would those be?"

"Certainly, the spy community. Of course, your reputation was slightly tarnished by your shenanigans in London. But I see you've been pardoned by the king himself."

"I didn't think one could tarnish a spy's reputation," Phoe snarked. "After all, a good spy shouldn't have one, right?" She arched her eyebrow and hoped that the woman understood the innuendo.

"True enough, I suppose. But the vampire covens all know him well."

"Oh?" Phoe looked to Cage. "And is that where you heard of him?"

The woman barked with strange, high-pitched laughter. "You think me a vampire?"

"Well, you consort with them," Cage asserted. "Perhaps you're Vlad's babydoll."

"Funny," the woman deadpanned. "But no. Cage is kind of a scary story among the covens. Before he got cozy with the IU again, he managed to make quite a name for himself hunting his own kind."

"They were never my own kind," Cage growled, his eyes narrow and cold.

The woman ignored his venom and continued. "St. John and his super-DNA could take out whole nests by himself. His high-paying clients could use him as their weapon, taking down vampires who had allegedly eaten family members or stolen their money. And his methods were... creative, to say the least. I believe that's how Maurice wiggled his way back into your life to start with, right?"

"What is she talking about?" Phoe asked. She stopped dead in her tracks.

"Oh, he never told you about his private assassin work?"

"Maurice posed as a client," Cage answered, gritting his teeth. He was walking faster now, as if trying to outrun the words he was about to say. "He asked me to chase down a drone named Dagger to save his daughter. Which is how I ended up on the Maglev with you. End of story."

"Or is it?" the woman asked.

"Who the fuck are you, anyway?" Cage glared at the steward.

"That's a good question," the woman replied. "Today I'm the steward from the Maglev that saved your lives."

"We weren't doing too bad," Phoe noted.

"You weren't doing too great either."

The three fell into silence as they reached a narrow gravel road that Phoe hoped would lead them to town. She was reminded of the town in Nebraska where she and Cage had narrowly escaped a zombie horde. She shivered, remembering how the creatures had skittered along the walls at an unnatural speed, their teeth chattering. Though they were currently in an open area, she couldn't help but wonder if some monstrous thing would jump out from behind the nearest tree.

"You okay?" Cage asked, falling into step beside her. He took her hand and warmed it gently between his. "You look a bit knackered."

Phoe nodded. "I'm all right, I suppose. I have a bad feeling about all of this."

"What do you mean?"

"I mean that in case you missed it, we were attacked by genetically enhanced vampires," Phoe whisper-yelled. "I really don't think that was a coincidence or that they were passing through. And now we're stranded in the middle of nowhere, following a total stranger into the wilderness. Does none of this seem a little odd to you?"

Cage chuckled and squeezed her hand affectionately. "I agree, but I don't think there's much we can do about it. Try to relax, love."

"Relax? Before or after I comb the vampire goo out of my hair?"

Cage pulled out his eSlate and began typing furiously with his long, nimble fingers. A hologram of the terrain around them popped into view. He turned the image in his hand and tried to zoom in on the next town in an attempt to calculate their position.

"I wouldn't do that," the woman told him.

"What?"

"Use the triangulation on your eSlate."

"Why not?"

"The second you put in those coordinates, everyone on the continent will know where we are."

"I thought that was the point," Phoe said. "Besides, what do you mean by everyone?"

"Everyone meaning the IU. Meaning your boss."

"Good," Phoe replied. "Maurice could send some help."

The woman threw back her head and laughed. It was a barking, maniacal sound that didn't make Phoe feel one bit better about their situation. "When was Maurice Wilder ever a help?"

"You know Maurice?"

"Hmph," she grunted. "Let's say I know *of* him. His reputation precedes him. I know him enough to know that you can't trust a word that comes out of his mouth."

"Well, he is a spy," Phoe humphed.

They fell into another long silence as they plodded down the gravel road. Phoe couldn't help thinking that it was strange that they hadn't seen a single car since they left the crash site. To say that the forest valley around the Carpathians was remote was an understatement, but they hadn't seen so much as a wagon.

Finally, lights appeared ahead of them. Phoe nearly giggled with joy. She was tired and hungry. Not to mention that the tiny life growing inside her was pressing insistently on her bladder. The cold wasn't making things much better, and her feet were killing her. The old Phoe was starting to rear her whiny little head.

As they got closer they could see that the lights were not those of a quaint little cottage in the woods, but an enormous, black prowler that appeared over the horizon. Its bright halogen lamps swept back and forth as if looking for something.

"I think that might be our ride," Cage said, pointing to the car. He whistled and waved his arms, trying to draw the attention of the driver.

"Or the person here to kill us," Phoe grumbled.

The prowler came toward them, hovering over the road. It was long and black with sleek lines and a glossy surface that reflected the countryside. Phoe squinted, trying to see who was driving, but the windows were tinted so dark that she couldn't tell.

"Jesus, the man couldn't be inconspicuous if he tried." The woman rolled her eyes and sprinted toward the car.

The winged doors on the prowler opened with a whoosh and a man peeked out. "Need a ride, kids?"

The man who stood in the doorway, holding the door for them could only be Vladimir Antonescu. He was an impossibly tall beast of a man with shoulder-length black hair and a black suit that made him appear to be a shadow.

"Vlad," Cage called. "It's about time you arrived, mate."

"The traffic was murder. Someone derailed a Maglev." He glared at Cage, flashing his vampire eyes. Then he smiled and gestured for them to come into the car. "I trust I left you in good hands."

The woman stepped up, holding out her hand. "I've fulfilled my purpose. My payment?"

"Of course," he replied, passing her a bundle of bills poised between his fingers.

She flipped through the money quickly. "We agreed on eight," she said. "I brought them to you unharmed as requested and I expect to be paid in full, vampire." Her hand was on the butt of the pistol at her hip.

Vlad smirked. "Easy, Natalya. Merely wanted to see if you were paying attention." He peeled another bill from his wallet and handed it over. She jerked it from his hand and pushed back from the door. As soon as her feet hit the gravel, she ran off down the road and disappeared into the forest.

"Isn't she coming with us?" Phoe asked. She hoped that her voice didn't sound as hopeful as she thought.

"Natalya? Of course not. She's not much of a people person. But do not fear for her. She's a bit of a monster in the dark herself." Vladimir held out a hand to Phoe. "Please, come aboard." He paused as a high-pitched screech sounded in the distance. "This is no place for long conversations."

Phoe glanced toward Cage. Vlad's thick, Slavic accent was like something out of a B-grade movie. "Thank you," she said, taking his hand. When he bent down and brushed his lips lightly over her knuckles, she nearly giggled as her cheeks flushed. Something about him was so seductive.

Vlad helped her step up into the prowler as it hovered a few feet over the road. "Such a pleasure to meet you, Miss Addison. I see the reports of your beauty hardly did you justice."

Cage took Phoe's hand from Vlad. "Could you get us out of here please?"

Vlad grinned, showing the delicate points of his fangs before sitting down across from them. He barked an order in his own strange tongue and the prowler began to rise. It was then that Phoe realized that unlike most prowlers, this one had no driver. In fact, the inside was more like a space cruiser than a car. It was spacious with a round seating area surrounded by a variety of buttons. In front of the passenger seats was a place for a driver, if, she supposed, they wanted one.

"I see you're still benefitting from the Quorti's generosity," Cage said. A hint of contempt colored his tone and Phoe pinched his side.

"And I see you're still playing at being a government lapdog."

"If by lapdog you mean not profiting from the suffering of others…"

"Some deserve to suffer, Macijah."

Phoe lay a calming hand on Cage's shoulder. "Come now, boys. Let us not argue." She could feel Cage's blood boiling beneath his skin. Earlier, he'd given in completely to the monster within and it was going to take a while for him to come down. If he was pushed too far, Phoe wasn't certain that she could pull him back.

"Miss Addison is right," Vlad said, his voice returning to the rich, smooth timbre from before.

"Phoe, please."

"Phoe." His smile was warm and his gaze piercing. So much so that Phoe found she had to look away. The vampire had a strange, rugged beauty. His longish black hair was wavy and thick. A single plait held it away from a pair of deep brown eyes that glowed with a red flame from within. His mouth was full, and she found herself watching the way his lips formed the words as he spoke. Everything about him was too large—his hands, his head, his jawline—but it gave him a beastly quality that she would have found enticing if Cage weren't at her side.

"My home is not far away. You'll take refuge for the night. You're weary and need to rest. I have much to tell you."

"Thank you, old friend," Cage said. "We hadn't expected to be attacked."

"I'm afraid my subjects may have been a bit overeager."

"Your subjects?" Phoe asked. "What does that mean?"

"Vladimir is the Carpathian King," Cage said.

"Descended from the Impaler himself." Vlad dipped his chin then poured himself a tumbler of a dark substance that looked mysteriously like blood. "Or so they say."

"That's interesting," Phoe started. "I'm afraid we missed you at the Gathering in Las Vegas last year."

"Before my ascension," Vlad explained. "Many things have changed in the covens since then. As you're no doubt aware."

"Somehow, I don't think those drones were friends of yours," Cage interrupted, anxious to change the subject. "There was something… off about them."

"Oh?"

"They were—physically deformed," Phoe interjected. "They seemed more animal than human."

"And they were able to create disciples instantly," Cage added. "One bite and the humans were infected."

"Impossible," Vlad stated, glancing away from them. "The human would have to drink of their creator's blood and then die, only to be raised again. That's how it works."

"I thought so too," Cage agreed. "But I saw them with my own eyes. Within seconds of the bite, the newborn was up and ready to fight. Ready to feed. Your friend seemed to know a little about them. Something about the *eshar* serum, perhaps?"

Vlad's expression was stoic, but Phoe could tell he was shocked by the revelation. "The serum is definitely dangerous, but to say that it's creating super-drones is a bit farfetched."

Phoe glanced at Cage. It was obvious he didn't believe Vlad either.

The vampire knew something that he wasn't yet willing to share.

Fifteen

The prowler came to a halt, setting down with a shudder. The door opened onto the courtyard of a massive castle, hulking and ominous in the fading light. Vlad started toward Phoe, but Cage was quick to her side. She tried not to let her mouth hang open as she took in the surroundings.

It was like something out of a dark fairy tale—an isolated castle, the Carpathian Mountains looming eerily around it. The mountaintops were already blanketed with snow, and even though it was barely November, the air was cutting as it whipped around her cheeks. A crumbling stone staircase rose up in front of them, leading to the entrance to the castle, which appeared to be carved out of the mountain. Aside from the narrow, twisting pass that had brought them here and the courtyard where they now stood, everything else fell away into a steep ravine below. Out of the corner of her eye, Phoe could see another jagged set of stairs leading down the hillside. In the distance, she could hear the thunder of rushing water.

"Terribly gauche, isn't it?"

"It's breathtaking." Phoe sighed dreamily.

"Indeed," Vlad replied. "Of course, a vampire living in the heart of the Carpathians is ridiculous."

"To say the least," Cage grumbled.

"One mad Irishman with a vivid imagination and a penchant for absinthe and here we are. Still, it's home."

The inside of the castle was almost as impressive as the outside. While it had a definite medieval vibe, modern fixtures gave it a brighter and less claustrophobic atmosphere. High, exposed beams, a spiraling staircase that led to the next floor, and heavy tapestries were offset by floor-to-ceiling windows that offered gorgeous panoramic views of the Carpathians.

"Surprised that there's no blood fountain?" Vlad teased, standing over Phoe's shoulder.

"Not at all," she said. "It's so beautiful."

"Would you believe that it was falling down when I bought it from the National Museum?"

"You've done a beautiful job restoring it."

"Dig up some Romani workers, Vlad?" Cage asked, sarcasm dripping in his tone.

"Of course. I lie in a box of dirt in my basement too. Keeps my complexion fresh. At any rate, there's a guest room already made up for you at the top of the stairs. I assumed that you'd only need one room?" He arched an eyebrow with such a wolfish expression that Phoe felt herself blushing clear down to her toes.

"One room will be fine," Cage acknowledged through gritted teeth.

Vlad crossed to Phoe and took her hand. He made a big show of bowing low and cradling it gently in his. "Feel free to avail yourself of anything I can offer."

Phoe could feel herself turning red. She had the strangest feeling that Vlad was almost hypnotizing her with the rhythm of his voice and the endless pools of flame in his eyes. It made her feel lightheaded, a bit like she'd felt when Eve had control of her mind through the port. It was an uncomfortable feeling, as if she were a marionette, but also exhilarating. "A warm bath where I can wash the vampire guts out of my hair would be fantastic."

"Of course," Vlad replied, unbothered. He kissed her hand again. She pulled it away from him and glanced toward Cage. She could see that he was ready to shift and completely annihilate Vlad, old friend or no.

"You're too kind," Phoe said.

"Entirely too kind," Cage grumbled.

Phoe smiled and started up the stairs. No way was she going to stand around and wait for the battle to start.

***

The two men watched Phoe as she disappeared up the stairs. Cage glared at Vlad, knowing that the vampire was watching every subtle sway of her hips, memorizing every curve. Not that Cage could blame him. Phoe was a beautiful woman, but she was *his* beautiful woman and he wasn't about to share.

"She's charming, Macijah," Vlad said, crossing to a side table where a jeweled decanter was full of something dark. "I can see why you love her so." As soon as he opened the bottle, Cage could smell the rich, coppery scent of the blood. It made his mouth water. He hadn't had human blood in such a long time. "But to be honest, I'm a little surprised to see you in a relationship after Corinne."

"I am too."

He watched as Vlad poured two tumblers full of blood and offered one to Cage. It took all of his strength not to down the whole thing in one gulp. He hated this hunger that came with the Splice. Cage never considered himself a vampire, and was in fact insulted by the notion, but he couldn't deny the bloodlust.

He took a small sip from the glass. The slippery thickness coated his lips and he licked them clean before taking another sip, then another, until he was guzzling the precious human essence.

"Take it easy, friend. It's been a while since you've had the real thing."

"Yeah, a little," Cage said, finishing the glass. He followed Vlad into a sitting room. With a flick of Vlad's fingers, the fireplace ignited with a *whoosh*. "Nice trick," Cage noted. "Shame I didn't get all the useful tricks."

"Some things cannot be reproduced through science, I'm afraid." Vlad was one of those rare vampires that was a genuine descendant of the Sin'khari. Cage had no idea how old he was, only that he'd been working for MI6 since before Cage was born. He'd kept his secret for many years. Cage had only found out about Vlad's condition by accident. Their relationship was complicated, to say the least.

Vlad poured Cage another glass. "There you are. Drink up, my friend. You look like hell."

"I feel a bit like it too," Cage admitted. "The last several weeks have been stressful."

"Ah, yes. Poor Maurice nearly getting himself killed by parties unknown. Former agents dropping like flies."

"My personal life is almost more than I can stand these days."

The vampire laughed heartily, showing the points of his teeth. "Oh, to have such a personal life as yours, Cage. Not all of us have your beacon in the darkness." He jerked his head toward the stairs, indicating Phoe.

"She is an extraordinary woman."

"Mmm… evidently. But I fear for you, Macijah."

"Why?"

"The last time you had a personal life, it ended badly."

Cage nodded. "I've learned from my mistakes. I turned Corinne into this delicate thing, and put her away on a shelf that I wanted to hide from the world. I thought that I could keep her separate from this life, but now I realize how wrong that was."

"Luckily you found someone willing to take this leap with you." Vlad sipped from his glass, then held it up to the light so that it cast a red reflection across his face. "I must say I'm envious. A woman like that could make a man think about retirement."

"You know I can't stand still." Cage was quick to answer, but he didn't believe it. Recently, the thought of taking Phoe and their children on a permanent vacation was extremely attractive. When that drone was attempting to tear Cage's head from his shoulders, all he could think about was his child being born without a father. Her could hear Phoe's voice in his mind, quivering and practiced as she called Ben to tell him that Cage wouldn't be picking him up for school holidays. With Corinne, he'd believed that he could carry on as before, but that was folly. A family changed everything. His life was no longer his own and he had to find a way to reconcile that fact.

"Seeing as how you're still gainfully employed by the Interplanetary Union," Vlad commented, "I'd guessed. Now, my friend, what are you doing here?"

"I need your expertise."

"I'm flattered."

"Seriously, Vlad. I know that you have a long history and an excellent memory. Especially when it comes to Others. And that you have connections within the covens. I need to know what you know about skin walkers."

Vlad's eyes grew large for a moment and then gave a dismissive wave. "I know that there's a legend about witches that could wear the skin of animals to take their shape. A scary story meant to keep children in their beds."

"I find it strange that you are so quick to discount the stories, considering that you yourself are a scary story."

"I'm not discounting, Cage, but I sense that there's more that you aren't telling me."

Cage sighed. He didn't know how much he wanted to tell Vlad about their adventures so far. It was true that he considered them friends, but Vlad was a vampire. Which meant that he couldn't be trusted absolutely.

"We think that whomever attacked Maurice is a skin walker."

"Intriguing. I've never met a real one."

Cage pulled out his eSlate and pulled up the footage from the party. "This is the only picture of the shooter we have. Phoe saw his face and I recognized him as an agent called Damian Lasko. He was part of a team that infiltrated vampire covens years ago, not long after the IU became aware of them. But he'd been inactive for years."

"How can you be sure that he's a skin walker?"

"We found this." Cage pulled up the photographs of Lasko's skin lying limp on the bed of the slum hotel.

"Ah, so he *used* to be a skin walker."

He swiped to the picture of Maurice's bullet wound. "There's also this. Maurice wasn't shot with your regular, run-of-the-mill autopistol. It's a slow-burn. A new type of weapon that kills the victim slowly by poisoning their blood. Whoever shot him is connected to someone with access to experimental tech. And everyone knows that black market tech is run by the covens."

"Which is where I come in, right?"

"Exactly."

Vlad stood and began to pace in front of the fireplace. His height and stature threw enormous shadows over the walls, nearly enveloping Cage in darkness. Finally, he spoke. "I may know someone who can help you. Assuming he'll be willing."

"What do you mean by that?"

"This man has made enemies within the covens."

"But he's loyal to you?"

"I wouldn't go that far, but he owes me." He pulled a small sphere from his pocket and placed it on the table in front of them. Silent footage began to play from it. Vlad waved his hand and the video stopped on an older man with spiked white hair and a sharklike complexion. "His name is Dr. Roland Gadeaux. He used to work for MI Six in their R and D department. He was dismissed several years ago after he did some unauthorized experimentation with genetic engineering."

"Unauthorized?"

"Real *Island of Dr. Moreau* stuff. Human-animal hybrids. Capturing Others and sampling their DNA to create all manner of things. Creating a skin walker wouldn't have been beyond the realm of possibility for someone like Gadeaux."

"And we know how the government is so squeamish about such atrocities," Cage noted sarcastically.

"At any rate, when they found out what he was up to, they tossed him out and stripped his credentials. Of course, the covens were all too eager to take him on."

"Why am I not surprised that vampires would be in league with mad scientists? It's like a terrible gothic romance. Paging Mary Shelley."

"Don't be so holier than thou. You're a bit of a science project yourself. Oliver Manning's splicing serum was merely the evolution of Gadeaux's work. Problem is, he was always more of a sadist than a scientist. Personally, I think the only reason MI Six was annoyed was because he got caught."

"I'm not so naïve as to think that this man will help us." Cage sighed. He could only hope that he hadn't dragged them out here and put their lives in danger for nothing.

"Trust me. He'll talk." Vlad flashed his vampire eyes and offered a grin so evil and sly that it made Cage shudder.

Sixteen

Phoe climbed out of the tub clumsily. She couldn't quite get the hang of this new center of gravity. She'd gotten through her first trimester like a champ. Sure, she'd been sick and had absolutely no sex drive, but this whole thing with Maurice and trying desperately to prove that she wasn't an invalid had managed to distract her sufficiently. But Mother Nature had a sick sense of humor. Now that Phoe was a ball of oversexed hormones, she looked like hell.

She gazed at her nude form in the foggy mirror. Stretch marks had already started to snake across her hips and she could barely see the tips of her toes when she looked down. Her breasts were disturbingly large with alien nipples that always seemed to be agonizingly hard. The book she was reading on her eSlate said that she should look to start leaking from every orifice any day now.

So yeah, the perfect time to get horny.

The door to the bedroom creaked open and she glanced around the doorframe of the tiny bathroom. Cage strolled in looking all glowy and strong. Evidently, Vlad had taken him on a hunt. She decided not to think about that. Everything about this place indicated that there were most likely villagers to feast on.

God, but Cage was so beautiful. Suddenly, Phoe felt bad about the late-night-telly thoughts she'd been having about Vlad. How could she possibly ever want anyone else? Everything about Cage, while not flawless, was perfect to her. His quick temper reflected his passionate nature. He took charge in every situation, which was a lovely balance to Phoe, who was often indecisive. His body was scarred, but each one told a story. They were a perfect match, and she was certain that deciding to marry him was the best decision she ever made.

She went to reach for a towel on the shelf by the tub, but Cage stopped her hand. Sidling up behind her, he took her wrist and draped her arm over his shoulder. She smiled, leaning back against him and inhaling his scent. She'd heard so many horror stories about women who were repulsed by the smell of their mate while pregnant, but this was not true for Phoe at all. Cage had a scent of leather, tobacco, and a hint of bourbon. It never failed to enflame her senses.

"You're going to catch cold," he whispered against her ear. His breath was moist against the shell of her ear.

She opened her eyes, watching him in their reflection. "You know that's an old wives' tale. You can't catch a cold from being in a cold place."

"Don't be so literal," he scolded. He wound his arms around her waist and pulled her tightly against him. She could already feel the hard knot of his cock pressing against the small of her back. He'd definitely had human blood. It always made him frisky.

Cage nuzzled against her neck. He sniffed her skin like he might be a wild animal. It was unusual and sexy. He pulled her hair away from her shoulder and brushed his lips along the slope. His hands moved along her hips and then over the gentle curve of her baby bump, now more pronounced, and lingered there. She shivered as the pads of his fingers played along the stretched skin. Every inch of her body was a bundle of nerves these days. Even the slightest touch made her gasp.

"You're so scrumptious, Miss Addison. I want to devour every morsel."

"Aww… you're only saying that because your friend was hitting on me."

He nipped her with the edge of his fangs, still partially extended from the earlier fight. "You could have looked less interested, you know."

"Oh, whatever do you mean?"

Cage gripped her hip tight and turned her around to face him. He had her cornered, her naked body pressed against the cool porcelain of the sink. "I think you know exactly what I mean."

"Ooo… jealous?"

He answered her question by grabbing her breast and kneading it gently, watching the nipple bead to a hard point. He slid down to one knee and took her center into his mouth. She couldn't help the tiny whimper that escaped her lips. Her skin prickled and for a moment she was sure her knees would buckle. Every sensation was so intense. As he pulled back, she could see the tiny drops of blood at the corners of his mouth. "I don't have to be," he snarled.

"Really?"

"You're mine. End of story."

Phoe purred at this alpha behavior. It didn't happen often, but when it did, it ignited an animal desire that made her want to push and tease. "I must admit that Vlad is kind of appealing to my more primal self."

"He'd eat you alive," Cage growled, nuzzling the inside of her thigh.

"I certainly hope so." Her voice trailed off in a guttural moan as he bit down at the junction where her leg met her pelvis. His fangs pierced the vein there and he suckled gently, careful not to drink too much. The baby didn't allow them to be reckless.

A curious thing happened when a vampire fed. The venom not only thinned the blood and allowed it to flow more freely, but once it got into the system, the prey experienced a euphoria that was almost orgasmic. That was probably the cruelest part of the kill—the victim wanted it.

Cage pulled himself away and Phoe swooned into his arms. "Take me to bed, vampire," she whispered, wrapping her arms around his neck.

He slid his hands under her bare bottom and hoisted her higher. She wrapped her legs around his torso, wanting to keep him as close as possible. She crushed her mouth against his as he carried her out of the bathroom and into the bedroom. Their kiss was furious, as if it would be their last. Phoe's lips felt swollen as they brushed against his cheeks and chin, savoring the coarse friction.

When they reached the bed, she slid down his body and sat down with a slight bounce. She began to fumble with the button on his pants. It was giving her more trouble than she was expecting until she finally tore them open with a loud ripping sound.

"Damn, Phoe. I liked those pants."

"Shush," she urged, pushing herself back on the bed. "Get them off and get over here."

"Yes, ma'am."

He shoved the pants the rest of the way down and kicked them aside. Phoe's mouth began to water as she stared. His skin, normally so pale, was flushed with heat and fresh blood. His eyes were sparkling in a way she'd only seen in a particularly satisfying fight. Tonight, he was holding on to the beast.

As soon as he hit the bed, the two of them slammed into one another as if they'd been waiting on this moment for years. Was it the ominous beauty of their surroundings, the afterglow of battle, or the encounter with Vlad that fueled this passion? She wasn't sure, but she wanted it to go on. When he released her kiss, she attacked again until they were both fighting for the next breath.

Cage rolled on top of her, pinning her arms above her head. He held her tight, and that little bit of pain was exhilarating. She arched her back, raising her hips insistently. He lapped at the tiny wound that still dribbled beads of blood down her thigh, carefully avoiding her sex. She groaned softly and wrapped a leg around his waist. She wanted to pull him inside, but he wasn't having it. Cage enjoyed the tease, making her crazed with desire until she was ready to scream was his favorite torment. But tonight, she wasn't in the mood for playing games. She wanted him to fuck her fast and hard and right now.

She hooked her leg around his and shoved against him with all of her weight. The sudden jerk knocked him off balance and she pushed him over on his back. He growled, trying to regain his dominance, but it was of little use. The phoenix burned under her skin and she used its strength to hold him down. She climbed atop him, crouching over him like a wild animal.

"Your skin is so hot," he breathed. "Am I in danger of going down in flames?"

She smiled and ran her fingertips along his belly, throwing sparks in the darkness. Crawling up his body, she consumed him, leaving white-hot kisses in her wake. When she reached his mouth, she whispered, "I only burn for you." He tried to kiss her, but she wouldn't let him get close.

She straddled his hips. She could feel his cock pulsing and growing as if it were reaching for the warm depths of her sex as she hovered out of range. She could feel tiny drops of her desire dripping down her thighs and lighting in the soft down at the base of his cock. She reached between them, taking him into her hand and squeezing lightly, offering a gentle pulse in slow rhythm that would make him sigh and purr beneath her. Their slick essences mingled, and soon he was arching into her hand.

"Fucking hell, woman," Cage growled. His eyes glowed with that unnatural light characteristic of the vampire. She smiled and raised up slightly, pressing the tip of his cock against her clit. She slid it up and down, teasing him as well as herself. Then, she let a little of him slip into her opening as she rolled her hips. Cage whined something unintelligible and she felt smug.

"Losing at your own game, eh?" she rasped.

"Evil tease." He didn't sound like himself. His voice was low and gravelly, more animal than human.

"Am I supposed to feel sorry for you?"

"I won't beg."

"I'd never ask you to," she purred, then slipped down, letting her sex devour him in one swift stroke. She gasped at taking him into her so deeply and so quickly. Evidently, he was surprised too, staring up at her with wide eyes. His surprise didn't last long, as she began to move, slowly at first and then speeding up, finding a faster rhythm.

Phoe balanced herself atop him then gazed down, and their eyes met. He grasped her hand and brought it to his mouth, kissing her wrist and then her fingers. One by one he nibbled at the tips then placed her hand over his heart. She could feel it beating, strong and sure. That was the one thing that with all Vlad's sexiness and supernatural mind tricks, he could never achieve. Cage was warm. Thick, hot, human blood rushed in those veins beneath his skin. His heart beat in time with hers, and when she kissed him, she could feel it quicken. He was alive, and this connection they shared was so much more than physical.

She could feel her eyes sting as she thought on this.

Her soul called out to his and he sat up and wrapped his arms around her. There was no movement, no sound. Their bodies locked together, as close as two people could be. She lay her head on his shoulder and let the tears fall on his shoulder, wetting his skin.

There was no sadness.

Only love and pleasure, and peace.

Seventeen

They had been driving across miles of what Cage assumed were goat paths for hours. Vlad had insisted that they take a traditional car so as not to attract attention. Cage couldn't argue. That half-prowler, half-spaceship monstrosity of Vlad's was definitely not inconspicuous.

The future had not caught up with this part of the world. Cage had the feeling that Vlad liked it that way. Most of the true Sin'khari did. They didn't want to draw too much attention to their kind, unlike the drones who wore their vampirism like a badge of honor. Most tended to forget that the Sin'khari were first and foremost scientists. Scholars who lived in solitude with their books until their world was coming to an end and they were forced to save it. Cage suspected that he and Vlad were more alike than they had previously realized.

"Where are we going?" Phoe asked. She was wringing her hands and had been bouncing her foot ever since they got into the car. She was nervous this morning. When Cage tried questioning her, she'd only responded with a short "Nothing" and offered a wide, almost panicked smile.

But she looked good enough to eat. She dressed all in black in an attempt to hide her pregnant frame. Her dark hair was pulled back in a high ponytail and she wore a set of wide, dark sunglasses that completely obscured her eyes. She also made no attempt to hide the holster on her hip or the hilt of a small dagger in her boot.

"The city of Cluj," Vlad replied. "One of my associates assures me that Gadeaux is having lunch at a small pub at the east end of town. Under the radar, of course."

"Why is he hiding?" Phoe asked. "I thought he was under your protection."

"In a manner of speaking. I don't let his enemies kill him. For now, anyway."

"Why would he have enemies? Did he do something to the covens?"

"He stole a great deal of money from the London syndicates. Their king is a moron called Tristram."

Phoe and Cage burst into laughter. Vlad stared at them as if they'd taken leave of their senses while they leaned against one another, shaking with giggles. "Do you two mind telling me what's so funny?"

"We're quite familiar with Tristram," Cage answered.

"And he is a moron," Phoe finished.

"Anyway, Tristram and Gadeaux were a match made in heaven at one time. Gadeaux was more of a sadist than a scientist and Tristram admired that. The more I think on it, I'm fairly certain that your deformed drones were the product of a Gadeaux experiment."

"Typical," Cage scoffed.

"As we discussed, my friend, you are the second generation of those experiments."

"The problem is, the next generation doesn't seem as successful," Phoe noted.

"On the contrary. What you described seems to be exactly what they were trying to achieve. You see, most vampires, Ankhil included, seem to think of us as a master race. They see humans as a commodity to be consumed, no more than cows or pigs. Gadeaux was tasked with making this happen. He promised them a formula for creating drones that were completely subservient and would reproduce quickly."

"Why so quickly?"

"Ankhil's plan was to be able to infest and colonize whole cities in a matter of weeks."

"A vampire planet," Phoe guessed.

"Exactly."

"But I thought that's what their colony was for. When Phoe and I were at the last Gathering, they were talking about a Martian colony, Aduamet."

"It's an argument that's been plaguing the covens for decades. Ankhil is impatient. He won't be content with a place to hide until the humans die out, having been devoured by Others. Machine promised him—"

"Machine?" Phoe and Cage said in unison.

"What does he have to do with it?" Cage asked.

"Who do you assume gave all that money to Manticore to fund their research projects that gave birth to the colonies? A sniveling megalomaniac like Derek Machine didn't have all that money on his own. He got it from the Quorti. Once the Earth was devoid of 'desirables,' the vampires would be free to pick off the rabble."

Something about this wasn't right. Cage was sure of it. There was something that Vlad wasn't telling them. He started to question further when the car came to a halt outside a shabby brownstone with a crumbling brick façade. There was a blue awning with the words *The River Maiden* painted sloppily across the front.

When they got out of the car, Cage took Phoe's hand and held it tight. He was fighting the urge to ask her to stay behind. She was an accomplished agent and there was no reason to assume that she couldn't take care of herself—but he couldn't help wanting to protect her.

And he had a bad feeling about this place.

"Gadeaux may have a couple of bodyguards with him. Possibly weres, so be careful."

"I thought you and this guy were friends," Phoe said, pulling an autopistol from the holster at her back.

"Friend is a relative term. Stay sharp."

The three of them walked into The River Maiden, trying to look inconspicuous. It wasn't an easy task. The room was dark save for tiny pinpoints of light coming from candles in the middle of the tables. There weren't many people, only a few tables of smarmy-looking characters talking in low tones. Their cigarettes created a dirty cloud that was almost impossible to penetrate as they walked through. There was a small stage at one end of the room where a bored topless dancer swung herself around on a rickety pole.

"I thought you said this was a pub," Phoe grumbled, pulling off her glasses.

"Some people like bare breasts with their lager," Cage deadpanned. Not that the girl on stage had much to offer in that department.

"Careful," Vlad warned, ignoring their conversation. "There are eyes everywhere."

A man that could only be Roland Gadeaux sat at a small table close to the stage. A stumpy, greasy lump of a man, he had an unhealthy growth of black fuzz around his head. One stubby hand clutched a cigar. He rolled it between his fingers in an almost obscene fashion. The other hand held a highball glass full of brown liquid. As the woman bent over, showing off her assets, Gadeaux catcalled and whistled.

"Show it to me, baby," he shouted. His speech was heavily accented, and Cage could see the saliva spray as he spoke. *"Vos seins sont comme des fruits mûrs. Je veux les mordre."*

"Well, he's charming," Phoe snarked, glancing at her companions.

"We're not here to make friends," Cage told her.

The three of them approached the table, and as soon as Gadeaux saw Vlad, the slimy scientist scrambled to his feet. With a small gesture, Vlad pulled the chair back against of the man's legs, forcing him to sit down hard. "Have a seat and stay a while, my friend."

"Look, Antonescu, I don't want any trouble with you," Gadeaux sniveled. He tossed his cigar into his glass and tried to get up again. Phoe pushed him down with her hands on his shoulders. Every now and then the phoenix strength came in handy. "Or your friends."

"You would do well to remember that you're only alive because I wish it, Gadeaux." Vlad flashed his vampire eyes and the man cowered.

"You misunderstand, my king. I am grateful for your protection."

"Do stop blubbering, Gadeaux." Vlad sighed. He waved to the waiter, who brought over a decanter of synthetic blood. Cage could tell by the way the light filtered through it. The waiter set the concoction in the center of the table along with three glasses. Obviously, he assumed that all of them were vampires. "We've come to ask some questions."

The grease ball gave Cage and Phoe a suspicious once over. "Who is we? I know nothing."

"That isn't the story that we heard," Phoe said. She leaned forward, took one of the glasses, and poured some of the synthetic. Her stare didn't waver from his as she downed the liquid. "This is a good vintage," she noted, replacing the glass and wiping the corner of her mouth with a delicate fingertip. "Not as tasty as the real thing though." She grinned, looking pointedly at Gadeaux.

"It's quite simple, Doctor," Vlad began. "I keep the Quorti from using your neck as a beer keg and you do whatever the fuck I want you to do."

Gadeaux reached for the bottle of cheap whiskey in front of him. His hand shook as he tried to pour out a glass. He only succeeded in getting half the glass filled before dropping the bottle. It made a clinking sound as it hit the floor and rolled toward the stage. The stripper stopped, looking annoyed that her patrons' attentions had been stolen. "Irina. Go." Gadeaux waved her away as he brought the glass to his lips. He slurped up the whiskey and slammed the glass down. "All right. *Posez vos questions.* But hurry up about it. *Il y a des yeux partout.*"

"My friend and I were attacked on a train traveling from Bargau," Cage said. "By vampires."

Gadeaux barked a bitter snicker. "The Bargau road is a place of legend. Many creatures of the night tend to prey on its travelers. And your brethren are known for turning on their own kind."

"They aren't our kind," Phoe stated. "These vampires were not... natural."

"There is nothing natural about them. Filthy, soulless demons."

He didn't get the words out before Vlad was jerking him across the table by his dirty collar. Gadeaux dangled from the vampire's enormous hands like a marionette. "Watch your mouth, human."

"We are in public, Antonescu. Would you risk showing yourself?"

"Do you see anyone watching us?" Vlad snarled, his fangs growing and his eyes on fire.

Looking around, Cage noticed that none of the patrons seemed to be in the least bothered by Vlad's sudden violence. In fact, most of them seemed to be avoiding watching them at all. Even Irina the stripper had made herself scarce at the other end of the bar.

"Humanity is so arrogant. The people here are under my protection and I pay most of their salaries. They continue to be willfully ignorant of my status and I make sure that they live comfortably. I could tear your head off right now and use your spine for a swizzle stick and no one here would so much as bat an eyelash." With that Vlad threw him back down in his chair, nearly toppling it. "So, you might try avoiding making me angry."

"As I was saying." Gadeaux cleared his throat and took another drink. "It does not surprise me that vampires would be lurking around the road. This is a wild land with many wild things about." He avoided Vlad's gaze.

"There are stories," Phoe started. "About a race of engineered drones. Drones that you helped Ankhil create."

The man realized that there was little use lying at this point. He sighed and nodded. "They're called *sanguisuge*. But they should be called virus. That's what they are. The idea was that a single *sanguisuge* could enter an area and turn the entire population to a type of slave drone in a matter of days."

"Why would anyone want that?"

Gadeaux looked at Phoe as if she had taken leave of her senses. "An infinite army, my dear. The Quorti and his followers feel that they are the master race and that the rest of us are sub creatures in their service. With the ability to create such an army, there would be no one that could stand against them."

"That's ridiculous," Cage scoffed. This sounded too much like a more insane version of Derek Machine's plans for New London. Super soldiers that could take on any army. A weapon beyond imagination.

"Is it? The vampire covens have managed to gain a foothold in almost every government in every country across the globe, all the while denying their own existence and evacuating worthy citizens to off-world colonies. And I was not the only scientist working on secret projects for the IU."

"The IU?" Phoe gasped. "You were working for them?"

"He worked for MI Six ages ago," Cage said, rolling his eyes.

"And the IU works for them," Gadeaux said, nodding toward Vlad.

"I think that's enough now." All of them turned at the voice that came like a wraith over their shoulders.

Derek Machine stood in the doorway of the pub, pointing a gun at the group. At least, they thought it was Machine. This man was different from the Machine that Cage had seen before. The Machine who had met him at the house in the middle of nowhere had looked on the edge of death. This man was fully alive and ready to take his revenge.

"You?" Phoe cried, jumping up. Cage followed, pushing her behind him. "You came to us for help."

"And so you did help me," Machine replied, his voice as serpentine as ever as he stepped into the room. "I found exactly who I was looking for." He looked around the room, the end of the gun still trained on them. "My king," he said with a sarcastic sneer to Vlad. "You should tell your subjects to retire for the evening." When Vlad made no move, he fired the gun in the air and the people in the pub began to scatter.

Gadeaux started to his feet, but Vlad pushed him down with a heavy hand on his shoulder. "Not you, asshole."

"Look, Machine," Cage argued. "If you've come here for revenge—"

"I have," Machine stated. "But have no fear. I didn't come here for you. It's taken me a long time to get this far. I had almost thought that all hope of ever finding him was lost. Then my old friends arrived and led me here."

"Fine. You win," Cage said. "But your quarrel is with me. Leave the rest of them out of it." Cage stepped forward. He could feel his Walther hanging heavily at his side. He needed a small distraction and he could take Machine down. This time Cage would be sure to kill the bastard so he could never bother them again.

"With you?" Machine asked. He threw back his head and laughed long and hard. Cage pulled his gun, but Machine fired first. His bullet grazed the back of Cage's hand and he dropped the gun. "Not so fast, St. John."

Phoe rushed to Cage's side, taking his hand. "What do you want?"

"My quarrel is not with you and your precious Macijah, Miss Addison. Though, lord knows I have enough motive. No, who I'm interested in is Dr. Gadeaux."

"*Moi?*" Gadeaux asked, squirming in Vlad's grasp. "I've never been anything but a friend to Manticore Industries."

"Ordinarily, I'd rejoice at one more sniveling bitch being put out of his misery." Vlad sighed, acting bored with the whole display. "But this time I really must protest, Mr. Machine." When he stood, several people that Cage had not noticed before stood up from tables around the room. "I'm not quite finished with the good doctor quite yet."

Machine grinned. "I really didn't want to do this, Vlad."

"Really? I've been waiting for centuries." In a flash, Vlad pulled his gun and a single shot rang out. Machine ducked, and the bullet shattered the wooden pillar behind. The noise ignited the rest of the bar and suddenly chaos ensued. Cage pushed Phoe aside as the windows facing the street erupted with Machine's minions pouring into the pub. Some of them were weres, others were mortals, but all of them had guns.

"Sorry, Phoe." Cage shrugged, then threw her backward toward the bar. She slid across the floor and out of the way. This was one fight she'd have to stay out of.

Cage pulled another gun from his hip holster and went down on one knee to grab the Walther. He fired twice, taking out two minions as they started through the window. He glanced to one side where Vlad was steadily picking them off one by one with every step. His servants turned over tables, using them for shields as they tried to hold off the advancing throng.

Cage couldn't be sure how many minions Machine had brought, but if they had been altered, there was no telling if they were mortal, undead, or if they could infect their allies in seconds as the creatures on the train had.

Something grabbed Cage from behind, leaping onto his back. It tried to pin his arms to his side, hissing and spitting in his ear as they struggled. The smell and the jerky movement of the creatures told Cage immediately that these were some of the *sanguisuge* like the ones from the train. They tried to bite at his neck and shoulders, crazed with their thirst. Cage struggled to raise up, bucking his body to throw them off before they could do too much damage. He turned to shoot them, but his balance was compromised with the weight of the creature and he went down on his back. Another threw itself on top of him, catching him by surprise. He fell backward on his arm and smacked the ball of his wrist joint against the floor. The shock loosened his grip on the gun and it fell away. He tried to raise the other arm, but another creature held fast.

Suddenly, a barstool flew from across the room and connected with the *sanguisuge* at the peak of his forehead. It made a gurgling noise and fell aside. Phoe stood over him with an angry expression on her face. Her whole body glowed an orangey red, and Cage could see the fire in her eyes.

"Don't shift," he shouted.

She grabbed the creature that still held Cage by the back of the head and raised him up with one arm. The thing dangled there briefly before she slammed it down against the nearest table, breaking the table and its back. "Don't tell me what to do," she growled, not sounding like herself at all. Another *sanguisuge* loomed behind her and she grabbed his face. Cage watched as the creature's face blackened and turned to flame as it screamed. She threw it aside and offered him her other hand.

Cage didn't have much time to look at her in awe before more of Machine's goons started shooting. He ducked, looking around frantically for his gun. Out of the corner of his eye, he could see the townspeople who were loyal to Vlad scattered around and bleeding from gunshot wounds. Cage grabbed Phoe and threw her over his shoulder, leaping over a table and then the bar, taking shelter. "We have to get out of here. There's too many."

"Not until I kill him," Phoe snarled.

"That's only valid if they don't kill you first," Vlad said, slamming into Cage's back. Another shot grazed Vlad's side and he peeked around the corner of the bar, firing three shots and dropping the shooter. "You two must have really pissed this guy off."

"Don't ask," Cage said.

"We should shift," Phoe argued. "We could get all of us out of here."

"You can't shift." Cage gritted his teeth and fired another round at the *sanguisuges*.

"Why can't she?" Vlad asked, breathless.

"She's pregnant," Cage shouted. "And I won't put our child in more danger." He winced as the glass bottles overhead exploded, raining shards down over their heads.

"Would you stop telling me what to do?" Phoe growled. "If we shift, we can get us, Vlad, and Gadeaux out of here."

"I don't think you have to worry about the good doctor," Vlad said, nodding to where a body lay by the bar, eyes open and staring out of the half of its head that was left.

And then the shooting stopped. Everything went eerily silent. The smell of gunpowder and cheap whiskey permeated everything, almost as heavy as the silence. There was a fog of smoke and Cage could scarcely breathe. His hand and arm were on fire, he supposed from the kick of the gun. Vlad slowly raised up, peeking over the bar, but was met with a shot that nearly took his head off.

"Shit," he hissed. "Still out there, I guess."

"Come on out, darlings. We won't bite" Machine laughed.

"Fuck you," Phoe shouted. "You got what you came for."

"Maybe I change my mind," he replied. "I've always wanted more."

Cage narrowed his eyes, listening closely. Machine's voice was strange and accented. It didn't sound like him at all.

"There's no way he's going to let us walk out of here," Vlad whispered.

"That isn't Machine," Cage said.

"What are you talking about? Of course it is."

Cage shook his head. "I know it sounds crazy, but that's not Derek Machine. The man I saw didn't have the strength to stage a shootout. Half of his body was mechanical."

"Could he have been playing with you?" Phoe asked.

Cage shook his head. "No. It isn't him. Besides, why would those *sanguisuges* be loyal to him? If what Gadeaux said was true, then those creatures are more monster than human. They'd have torn Machine apart like hungry animals."

Vlad nodded. "He's right. *Sanguisuges* only fight for blood."

"Tick-tock, boys and girls," Machine called. His voice was a high-pitched, sing-songing taunt. "There's no way out except through me, and by my calculation you're dangerously short on ammunition."

"And there's this," Cage said with a pained groan. He held up his hand that had been shot. The wound had a distinctive star-shape to it with a starburst pattern of bloodlines that ran up Cage's arm. Despite Cage's ability to heal, whatever had shot him was spreading a poison.

"Oh, God," Phoe whispered. "A slow-kill bullet. Like the one that nearly killed Maurice." She looked up at Vlad with fearful, pleading eyes. "We have to get Cage out of here before the poison spreads."

"I can shift," Cage said.

"No, you can't. Remember what Ollie told you? Shifting will only speed it up."

Vlad crouched and growled, stretching his neck as his fangs grew. He grabbed a gun from the holster at his back, cocking it. His eyes glowed and for a split second, Phoe was terrified of him. "Then let's get him out of here. Stay behind me."

Vlad came out from behind the bar with a roar. One of the *sanguisuges* ran at him immediately, attacking from the side. The monster grabbed Vlad by the arm he was using to shoot and twisted it behind him. "Let's go," Vlad shouted, pulling the creature in front of him. He used it like a shield as he made his way toward the door. He began to shoot through the dying monster, killing three more, until it was nothing but a ruined corpse. He threw it aside and the weight of the thing took out two more.

Another of Machine's minions screamed, coming at Vlad swinging two large machetes. Vlad ducked the blades as they slashed over and over. He finally managed to get his free hand around one of the creature's arms and pulled it close, pressing the barrel of the gun against its side and shot four times in rapid succession as they moved forward. He threw that one aside and grabbed another, pulling it close and sinking his teeth into its throat. He drained it in seconds before throwing it aside.

Phoe pulled Cage along behind her. He was getting weaker by the second and she wouldn't be able to support his weight much longer. "Phoe… I'm going to have to shift. It's the only way."

"No," she screamed. "The poison will kill you."

"I'm going to have to take that chance."

She started to respond, but her attention was drawn by something in the corner. Cage followed her gaze to where the Machine-thing was crouching in the corner. Such a fucking coward. Evidently, he was rethinking his strategy at witnessing Vlad's carnage. Not that Cage could blame him.

Machine crouched in the shadows, pulling his clothes off in a terrified frenzy. That would have been strange enough, but Cage realized that his body was contorting and shaking. It was almost like he was having a weird type of seizure. Perhaps he'd gotten a little too much of his own poison. Then, Machine covered his face with his hands. He began to pull at his hairline. The flesh there was odd, wrinkled and warped and loose. The skin began to peel away from his skull, leaving behind a bloody, distorted form. Under the gore was a leathery skin that was a transparent gray. Cage could almost see the veins and organs beneath it.

"What the fuck is that?" Phoe asked.

"I'm not sure," Cage answered.

The creatures must have seen this transformation as well. They made strange huffing noises and scattered, suddenly more afraid of this whatever-it-was than Vlad and his gun.

Vlad stopped, finally noticing that his opponents were running away. For a moment, Cage could tell that he was proud of himself for his ferocity that had evidently scared them off. Then he noticed the strange creature in the corner.

It threw Machine's skin off and ran out through the door.

Eighteen

"What in the hell was that?" Vlad asked, stomping on the gas pedal and speeding away from Cluj. "I've never seen anything like that." He was covered in blood and had a variety of slowly healing holes peppering his chest, but he seemed much more concerned with whatever that science experiment was that had run away from the pub.

"No idea," Phoe replied. And honestly, she didn't really give a shit right now. Cage lay across the back seat of the car with his head in her lap. She brushed her hand across his brow. He was burning up with fever and his pupils were blown out like a drug user. "And I honestly don't care. We have to get some help for Cage."

"Uh… there's a hospital when we get back to Brasov."

Phoe shook her head. "He's an Other. An Ultra. I'm not sure that a regular hospital will be able to help him. We have to slow the poison until I can get him to Ollie."

"I've never seen anything like that," Vlad repeated. "It was like a shape shifter."

"It was a skin walker," Cage said, his voice weak.

"What? How do you know that?" Phoe asked.

"He's hallucinating," Vlad answered. "He's burning up with fever. He doesn't know what he's saying. I told you before—the skin walker is a myth, nothing more."

"It isn't," Cage yelped as he tried to sit up. "You have to listen…"

Phoe held him, trying to keep his body still. "Shush, darling. We'll figure it out."

"You have to go back," Cage insisted, ignoring them. "Before it can change its form again."

"So, you think that the person you saw that night you went to Death's Door… you think that it was someone impersonating Machine… by wearing his skin?" Phoe asked.

"No," Cage answered. "I know that was Derek Machine. And I know that Machine is dead."

Vlad caught Phoe's eyes in the mirror. "Is he making any sense to you?"

"You have to believe me…" Cage murmured, his words drifting off, too weak to continue.

A lump began to form in the middle of Phoe's chest. She was trying to hold it together, but she couldn't help but think that Cage was dying right here in her arms.

Tears burned and she looked out the window at the dark trees rushing by as they drove back toward the castle. What would she do if he didn't make it? The thought of going back to St. Francisville alone, or worse, their flat in London, was more than she could take. She'd come to depend on him. She needed him in a way that she'd never needed another being in her whole life. If he left her now, Phoe didn't think she could go on.

When they reached the castle, Cage was unconscious. Judging by the color of his skin, the poison had traveled from his hand, up his arm and was spreading across his chest and into his throat. His hair was soaking wet and his cheek was so hot that it burned Phoe's hand to touch it.

"Come on, Phoe," Vlad coaxed. His voice was gentle. As gentle as a vampire's voice could be. "Let's get him inside. You'll call Oliver and perhaps he can tell us how to fix this mess."

Phoe nodded, unable to speak. She was afraid that if she said anything that she would start sobbing, and the last thing Cage needed right now was a hysterical woman sobbing over him. She needed a level head.

Vlad came around to the back and hoisted Cage out of the car and over his shoulder. She couldn't help being impressed. Cage was no featherweight, but Vlad had picked him up like he weighed nothing.

She followed Vlad into the house and up the spiraling staircase to the bedroom above. She already had her eSlate out and was punching Ollie's number. It rang a few times and then the voice messaging picked up.

"Damnit, Ollie," Phoe swore, breaking the connection. She tried twice more and still no answer. Then she had a thought and dialed Jess's number.

"Hello?"

Phoe almost laughed. She'd never been so glad to hear her sister's voice. "Jess, thank God."

"Hello? I can't hear you."

"Not that I don't want to talk to you, but is Ollie with you?"

"Oh wait, I'm not with my phone right now. You'll have to leave a message."

"Goddamnit, Jess," Phoe yelled, shoving the eSlate down into her pocket. "I hate it when she does shit like that."

The panic began to take hold as the adrenaline from the fight began to wane. This helpless feeling was not something she'd experienced in a long time. In fact, the last time she'd felt it was as she was sitting by her mother's bed, watching her die a little more each hour.

Toward the end, Phoe's mother's organs had begun to shut down. One of the symptoms was that toxins in her body built up and got into her brain, making her completely insane. She would scream and cry and nothing Phoe said or did would help. Then, her mother fell unconscious for a couple of days and Phoe hated herself for feeling relieved that she didn't have to sit by her mother's side trying to convince her that everything was all right.

Finally, on that last day, her mother had woken up and for a little while it seemed that she'd come back to her senses and everything was going to be okay. Then she looked at Phoe with a slight twinkle in her eye and said, "I know I'm still asleep. You're all just dreams." In that moment, Phoe had felt so completely helpless. None of the prayers, none of the medicine, none of the bargains with God had done a damn thing.

She felt that way now.

Phoe closed her eyes and took a few deep breaths, trying to steel herself before walking into the bedroom.

Vlad sat by the bed, a heavy glass decanter in his hand full of something dark and thick. Cage lay on the bed, still unconscious but breathing heavily. It was almost a pant. He had evidently pulled his shirt off as it lay in tatters on the floor at the foot of the bed. His body was covered with sweat, but he shivered as if they were still outside.

Phoe rushed to his side and sat down, taking his hand. His skin felt cold and clammy like a dead fish. "Is he dying?" she asked Vlad.

"I don't think so. But he is extremely ill. I've given him some human blood to see if that will speed his healing ability. I don't understand it. His wounds are almost completely healed but this poison lingers. How fitting that the assassin, whoever it was, would choose one of Gadeaux's own creations to kill him. And then, ironically, he was killed with a single bullet."

"Leaving my love to die," Phoe cried, her voice flat. She wanted to be angry, but right now she didn't have the strength.

Vlad reached out and patted Phoe's shoulder, attempting to comfort her. "He isn't going to die, Phoe."

"You don't know that."

"He is strong. He can fight this off. We have to give him time. Were you able to reach Dr. Manning?"

Phoe grunted. "Of course not. His eSlate keeps going to the voice message. Ollie hates the eSlate. He only has it because we give him such a hard time about it."

"He'll call you back."

"It might be too late by then." Phoe rose from the bed and began to pace around the room. So many emotions tumbled around in her head. It started to ache. "We should have left this life behind. He was willing, you know. Right after we met, before Maurice lured us both into BEAST. We could have had a simple, quiet life in St. Francisville."

"St. Francisville?"

Phoe nodded. "My hometown. Funny, I always wanted to leave it. Thought it was too small. Too humdrum for adventures. Everyone following a set routine. Nothing ever changing. Eight hours of work, then coming home for a nice dinner and maybe watching a holovid before bed. On the weekends going into New Orleans for a movie—the height of excitement." Phoe huffed and laughed bitterly. "I thought it was so stupid. I could never want a life like that."

"Sounds kind of nice," Vlad said.

"It does, doesn't it?" Phoe replied. "God, I'm so stupid."

Vlad went to her and she fell into his arms, relieved to have his strength to hold her up.

"Don't do that, Phoe. You should not have regrets for the life you've chosen. Each step has made you who you are."

"And who is that?" she sniffled. "Some helpless ninny. Sure, I can turn myself into a phoenix and take down bad guys with my bare hands, but I can't"—she threw out her arm—"save his life. Nothing I do can save him."

All at once the tears started to flow. The dam had broken and Phoe was sure that she'd never hold them back again. She was so angry with herself for going to pieces. Cage needed her to be strong, but this was too much. She sobbed against Vlad's shoulder for what seemed like hours. She sobbed until her shoulders ached with the exertion and her eyes felt gritty.

"Wait," Vlad said. He grabbed her by the shoulders and held her at arm's length. "Did you say you could change into a phoenix?"

Phoe sniffled. "Yes, but what has that got to do with anything?"

He grabbed her wrist and pulled her over to the bed. "Sit down."

"What?"

"Stop wasting those fucking tears on me and do something useful."

"What do you mean?"

Vlad rolled his eyes. "You're a phoenix, idiot."

"How is that useful?"

"I'm not usually up on my mythological studies, but I believe I remember something about phoenix tears having healing properties." He tipped her chin upward. "It's worth a try."

Phoe leaned over, kissing Cage's temple lightly. "I feel ridiculous," she whispered, then kissed his mouth. She glanced up at Vlad who stared down at her expectantly. She closed her eyes and said a small prayer that this would work. That she would still have enough tears to heal him. She opened his mouth and used her fingertip to gather some of the tears that clung to her cheeks. She brushed her fingers over his lips, spreading the salty liquid at the inside of his mouth. As she did this, his eyes began to flutter.

"I'd call that a response," Vlad stated.

Phoe smiled and to her surprise, tears sprung to her eyes again. She clutched her fist and dug her fingernails into the heels of her palms, hoping that the pain would bring more. It did and before she knew it, fat droplets of tears were dripping over her cheeks and into Cage's mouth. In seconds his breathing slowed and evened out. The heat emanating from his body seemed to subside, and she could see the poison beginning to recede.

"Look what you can do," Vlad said, laying a comforting hand on her shoulder.

A wave of relief rushed over her and she laughed. Cage was going to be okay.

"Oh, Cage." She sighed, kissing his forehead and eyelids. "Are you all right?"

"I think so…" he whispered. "What happened?"

"You were shot with a slow-kill slug," Vlad told him. "Machine shot you."

Cage tried to sit up, but he was still weak and fell back against the pillow. "It wasn't Machine."

"Take it easy, love," Phoe shushed, kissing his hand. "Lie still. Rest now and we'll figure out what to do in the morning."

"We have to find the skin walker before it gets away. It's going to go after Maurice again. I'm sure of it. He's the only one left."

"The only one left?" Vlad asked.

"The original MI Six team," Phoe explained. "Machine, Oded Nazari, Maurice, and Natalya Kristokoff. Oh wait… Natalya."

Vlad laughed. "Natalya Kristokoff? My Natalya Kristokoff?"

It suddenly dawned on Phoe that the woman who had saved their lives on the Maglev had been named Natalya. How stupid that she hadn't thought of it before now. "Oh my God."

Cage obviously followed her train of thought as the pieces started to click into place. "Vlad, where did you meet Natalya?"

He shrugged. "She showed up in the village asking questions about a year ago. I thought she was another babydoll looking for a vampire lover."

"Did she always look like that?"

"Like a woman? What do you mean?"

Phoe and Cage exchanged puzzled glances and she pulled out her eSlate again. She tapped the screen and said, "Search missing persons, female, Brasov, Romania." The projection pulled up a cabinet of photos showing women that had been reported missing in the area. "Filter by age twenty to thirty-five." The hologram flipped through several of the women, narrowing the list. Phoe clicked over them one by one.

"That's her," Vlad said, pointing at one of the women. He grabbed the hologram and pulled it out. "Ana Filotti."

"According to this news article, she was a waitress that disappeared about a year ago outside the restaurant where she worked in Bucharest."

"I'm willing to bet that if we searched her room in the village, that we'd find Miss Filotti's body," Phoe huffed, feeling stupid for not realizing this before. "Natalya is the skin walker."

"And she'll be going after Maurice next," Cage said. "And this time, she won't stop until he's dead."

Nineteen

"Tell me again why we aren't going back to London via Maglev?" Phoe shifted uncomfortably in the narrow seat of the shuttle plane. Her gaze moved back and forth, examining each of the people in the small cabin. Any of these people could be Natalya Kristokoff. And if there was going to be a fight, Phoe would much rather have it on the ground.

"It's the fastest way to get there," Cage replied with a groan. He'd taken only a day to recover—Phoe had been adamant that he rest—from the poisoning, and complained the whole time that it was likely a day too many. Vlad had given him all the Type O he could manage to harvest from his disciples, but Cage was still dragging. She didn't like to think about it, but the poison bullets from Natalya's gun had nearly killed him. "And we need to get to Maurice before Natalya does."

"You should have let me go back on my own," Phoe told him. "Vlad would have been glad for you to stay with him a couple more days."

"And miss all this fun?" Cage rolled his eyes as yet another passenger bashed his head with their carry-on luggage.

"I'm not sure you're up to this."

"Look," Cage began, "Natalya Kristokoff is a trained killer. I looked up her file in the MI Six database—she's a certified badass. When she went off the grid, the agency sent people after her. Most came back in body bags. All the others were never heard from again. She's no one to trifle with."

"Are you saying that I can't handle myself?" Phoe tried to keep a patient, even tone despite the fact that all this doubting was starting to piss her off. How long did they have to be partners before she gained his trust as an agent?

Cage turned and took her face between his hands, forcing her to look in his eyes. "Of course, I'm not. I would never say that." He leaned in and kissed her cheek then offered a wink. "I trained you myself. You're an exemplary spy."

"You don't think I can handle wet work. You think I'm too soft."

"That isn't it. I don't want you to get hurt." He placed a warm hand over her middle. "It isn't only ourselves to consider, you know."

Phoe nodded, agreeing with him. No one had officially said the words that she needed to retire from spy work when the baby arrived, but she knew that's what they all thought. This life was too dangerous for a mom. It wasn't like those sappy movies where the high-powered executive takes her baby to work in a modified backpack.

"You could have let me take Vlad," she mumbled, hiding the devious grin that slowly crossed her lips. "I'm sure he'd have been able to protect us quite well."

Cage huffed. "Despite your illusions about him, Vlad's no hero. He might be tall, dark, and handsome, but he is a vampire and therefore two-faced by nature. Make no mistake that if a better offer came around, Vlad would sell you to the highest bidder."

"Oh, you think everyone's evil."

"Most everyone is."

Phoe giggled and snuggled into the crook of his arm. "I know you don't really believe that."

"No?"

"Of course not. You're almost as optimistic about the future as I am."

"It's because my future is with you." Cage reached into his pocket and pulled out his eSlate. He began flipping through his messages.

Phoe watched as the rest of the passengers began filing into the plane. This was only a small shuttle, but the airline crammed as many people as possible into the plane. Usually this route was mostly business types travelling to meetings in Eastern Europe, but this particular flight had a variety of people, from older tourists to families with small children. Phoe spied a young woman out of the corner of her eye. She stared down at her boarding pass, then up at the tiny numbers over the seats. Her gaze went everywhere, and she looked terrified. Phoe grinned, remembering herself on that fateful Maglev trip more than two years ago.

"She needs a Cage," Phoe said, nudging Cage.

"Pardon?"

Phoe nodded toward the young girl as she dropped her luggage on the floor, spilling the contents all over the aisle and causing a backup. A man sitting on the aisle noticed her distress and stood up to help. "Oh… there he is. Her hero."

"Poor bastard," Cage murmured. "He should have pretended not to notice. Now he'll be stuck for good."

"Hey now." Phoe gave Cage her best glare. "I'm the best thing that ever happened to you." She looked up into his eyes, those endless pools of blue that always left her breathless.

"That you are, love." Their lips met in a long kiss that left Phoe wanting. "You're definitely the best."

He leaned in to kiss her again when a strange fluttering in the pit of Phoe's belly made her gasp. "Oooh…"

"What? Are you all right?"

She chuckled nervously. "Uh… yeah. I had the oddest feeling."

"What sort of feeling?"

As soon as Cage spoke, the fluttering happened again, this time it felt like a wave of tiny fingers on the inside of her stomach brushed across her middle. It wasn't painful, but she'd never felt anything like it. "I'm not sure, but—but I think the baby moved." As if in response, she felt a small thump, almost as if her internal organs rolled over, bumping into each other. "Oh my," she whispered. This time she did laugh and grabbed Cage's hand, pressing it against her midsection.

"Phoe, I don't think I'm going to feel anything," he said. He looked around as if the sight of him feeling around on his fiancée's tummy might disturb the other passengers. He forgot to feel self-conscious when the baby kicked so hard that it moved his hand. "Oh. Wow."

"See? I told you. Isn't it amazing?"

"It… wow." He stared down at her belly, watching it bulge slightly with every movement of their unborn child. "He's incredible."

"He? What about *she*? The baby might be a she you know."

He was so amazed that Phoe's heart swelled in her chest. Every time she didn't think she could love Cage more, he did something so adorable that she couldn't help falling in love all over again.

"Whatever it is, I love it already."

Phoe moved the armrest between them and snuggled into his side, holding his hand to her stomach. "I think she likes you. She moves every time you speak."

"I never got to feel Lily move like this," Cage murmured. "I was always gone. I wasn't even there when she was born. I got home in time to pick them up from the hospital. Corinne was pretty pissed."

"I'm sure she understood."

"I guess," Cage said. "Maybe eventually she did. Not that she should have. I was an incredible ass. I realize now that I put everything ahead of her and that was wrong, Phoe. It was wrong, and I won't do it again." He tipped her chin up to look down into her eyes. "There is nothing more important than you and our child. Children."

"What are you saying?"

"I'm saying that the answer to all of my apprehensions has been staring me in the face all this time." He shifted his body, turning toward her. "I didn't want to admit it because I thought it might somehow take away from who I am. But I'm going to do right by you, Phoe. By you and Ben and this child. After this job, I'm done."

"Done with what?"

"Done with BEAST. Done with the IU. Done with sneaking around and chasing after people, vampires, skin-walkers, and weird created things. I'm done."

Phoe's eyes widened and her heart began to pound. She couldn't believe what she was hearing. Had Cage really told her that he was ready to retire? "Are you serious? What about Maurice?"

"It doesn't matter what Maurice or anyone else wants," he said with a shrug. "I've been thinking about this a lot lately. My biggest mistake with Corinne was that I tried to keep my life with her separate. It was like she was a prized antique sitting on a shelf waiting for me." He took Phoe's hand in his, clasping it gently. His fingertips traced the tiny bones on the back as if trying to memorize every line. "She should have been the only life that mattered. Her and Lily. I don't want to miss that chance again."

Phoe's mouth hung slightly ajar as she tried to process what he was saying. "But what will we do?"

Cage laughed. "Whatever we want. I've had a long career and I'm always prepared, so money isn't an issue."

Phoe giggled. "You're telling me that you'd be perfectly content to live in St. Francisville. A quiet life with PTA meetings and tea on the porch with Miss Ava?"

"Or London. Or wherever we want. I mean, isn't there some dream that you've always had?"

She shrugged. "I don't really know. I mean... no one's ever asked me before."

"Well I'm asking."

Phoe could feel herself blushing. Funny that after all this time, that intensely blue gaze of his could still make her nervous. "I've always wanted to travel. I mean, someplace where I'm not going to be attacked by wild creatures that want to kill me."

"Okay. Where?"

"I don't know. Everywhere. The pyramids, the Amazon rainforest, one of those floating huts in Bora Bora."

Cage pulled her close, kissing her crown. "Anywhere you want to go."

"And then, when I was a kid, I always thought about opening a little coffee shop with a bookstore attached. I even found the perfect place for it in St. Francisville."

"So, let's do it. Let's go. We can take Ben out of that bloody school, adopt him for real, and go back to St. Francisville. Do the remodel on your mum's house that you've been wanting to do for years. Make a whole new life there."

Phoe unwrapped herself from his arms and turned to face him. "Where is this coming from? Retirement has been something you were against until this conversation. Are you like a pod person or something? Where's the real Cage?"

He snickered and shook his head, his curls bouncing over his forehead. "The other night, when I was lying there, and that poison was inside me, I could feel it killing me, my body dying. The coldness of it. And I opened my eyes and saw you there, crying over me, and I had a revelation. I decided right then that if I survived, that I would never make you cry again."

"But Cage, you love your work. You always have."

"I love you more. I love our unborn child more. I love Ben more."

She started to answer but found that the words wouldn't come. For the first time in her life, she'd been struck absolutely speechless. She had been waiting her whole life for someone to say these words to her. That she was the most important thing in someone's world. That someone was offering to take care of her for a change. She'd been fantasizing about this moment and now that it was here, she couldn't say a thing. "I—" She didn't get a chance to answer, interrupted by her eSlate buzzing.

She looked down. "It's a message from Maurice." Phoe showed Cage. A small wave of relief settled in. They'd been trying to get him to answer his slate all morning. It wasn't all that unusual for Maurice to be unreachable, but given the situation, they were nervous. "He says that he's safe, but that we need to get back to London ASAP."

"Good of him to tell us," Cage rolled his eyes. "Let him know we'll be back to HQ in a couple of hours."

"He's not at HQ," Phoe whispered as she looked up at Cage. "He's at Arrington. Ben's in danger."

Twenty

Arrington School was on a hill well outside London. The spires of the various towers and the expanse of green courtyards put Phoe in mind of knights and ladies that surely must have lived here more than a millennium ago. The sky above was gray, dreary, and spitting rain. The perfect day for mysterious adventures. Any other time she'd have been tempted to go exploring, but today the sight of the school filled her with dread.

"I can't believe he didn't say any more than that," Cage growled, pulling the prowler to a screeching halt in front of the school. "It's just like him to get us all worried and then not respond to any other messages."

There was something strange going on. Usually, when they came to visit Ben, the courtyard was full of students running back and forth, laughing and shouting, or studying under the enormous oaks that lined the quad. Today, there was nothing. It was completely dead. "I dunno, Cage. I don't think this is about Maurice's ego. I have a really bad feeling."

"You and your bad feelings," Cage chuffed, shoving the prowler's door open. He went around to the back of the car and pulled open the trunk. Inside was a virtual arsenal: autopistols, traditional guns, daggers, and even a couple of sticks that looked like electrified clubs.

"Damn, Cage. I don't think we're going to need all this."

"I like to have choices." He pulled out two pistols in addition to his favored Walther and a dagger, and handed them to Phoe. "Here."

"What is all this about?"

"You can't shift. You may need all the weapons you can get."

"I may not have a choice. It'll be fine."

She started to walk away, but Cage stopped her with a heavy hand on her shoulder. He turned her around, staring down into her eyes with a ferocity she didn't often see. "Please, Phoe. Don't take any unnecessary chances."

"No more than you."

He shook his head. "You and the baby are more important than me. Don't shift and don't take any chances." He gripped her arm tighter. There would be bruises later. "Please. You have to promise me."

"All right." She sighed, pulling away. "I promise I'll be careful."

"And that you won't shift."

His eyes were on fire. He looked so desperate. She could tell he was terrified. She'd never seen him this way, and honestly, it scared the shit out of her. "Okay, Cage. I promise."

He nodded and took off toward the main entrance. He pushed open the door and it flew back with a creaking bang as it hit the wall behind it. They walked in, expecting to be met with an angry headmaster, scolding them for barging inside, but there was no one. The main hall was deserted and there were scaffolds lining the east wall. "What the hell?" Cage murmured.

"Where is everyone?" Phoe asked.

"Maurice's message said Ben was here. It specifically said to come to Arrington."

"So it did." Cage and Phoe turned at the familiar voice of Maurice Wilder coming in behind them.

"Maurice? Is that you?" Phoe called.

"What's going on, Wilder?" Cage asked.

"I could ask you the same question. I got a message from you telling me to come to Arrington. That you were in trouble."

"We didn't send any message about Arrington," Cage stated. "But you are in danger, Maurice."

"So, if you didn't call us," Phoe started, "where is Ben?" Suddenly, they heard screaming from the floor above. Her heart lurched and the pain of it was almost paralyzing. "Oh my God," she breathed, glancing for a moment at Cage before they both took off up the stairs, nearly mowing Maurice down.

They moved quickly, guns drawn. They could hear Maurice's footsteps behind them, hot on their heels. The last time they'd played a game like this Eve Manning had nearly killed them. At least they were here on Earth instead of a Martian colony where she could make the rules.

They emerged at the top of the tower into a large, empty classroom. It was dusty and smelled strongly of mold. There was a window at the side that had been broken out, and the cold autumn breeze had scattered leaves across the floor. There, in front of it, tied to a chair, was Ben. "Oh God," Phoe shrieked, going toward him.

"Phoe. Cage. Help me," Ben screamed.

They ran to him, quickly trying to untie the knots that held him. "Ben, darling, who did this to you?" Phoe asked.

"I don't know," Ben whined. "I was walking down the breezeway, going to my math class and… I don't know, somebody hit me on the head. When I woke up, I was here."

"All right, love. We'll get you out of here."

"Cage," Ben cried. "Help me."

"Stay calm, Ben." Phoe tried to soothe him. "Everything's going to be okay."

Maurice stood on the other side of the room, wringing his hands. Phoe wanted to scream at him to help, but he looked like he was going to be sick. "I tried to stop you," he snapped. "I tried to keep you from this, but… you were both so persistent. If only you'd listened to me."

"What are you talking about?" Phoe asked. "Help us." Whoever had tied the bonds had known what they were doing. The metal-like cables that held him were tight and unforgiving. Even Phoe's dagger wasn't any help.

"The *sanguisuges*. The experiments. The vampires. I'm sure Vlad told you everything."

"Vlad only told us what we needed to know," Phoe replied. "And right now, I couldn't give a flying fig about weird experiments or government espionage. Help me free my child."

"There's no such thing as friends in this world, Phoe. Your lover there should know this."

"We wanted to help you," Cage said.

"He doesn't want any help." Phoe gasped as Derek Machine stepped through the entrance behind them, his gun trained. "And he doesn't want your friendship. He doesn't even know the meaning of the word."

"Derek?" All the color drained from Maurice's face. "Derek, I thought…"

"You thought I was dead. I can understand that, seeing as how you were the one holding the gun, standing over me. Watching as I bled out my last, gasping for breath and begging you to help me. I guess a thing like that tends to make an impression. And you," he said, turning to Cage. "I'm kind of surprised to see you here. Those slow kills usually work better than that. Still, I should be grateful. The poison gave me enough time to go back for my disguise."

"This can't be…" Maurice stumbled backward, away from Machine.

"It isn't," Cage growled. "That's not Derek Machine."

"He knows that. Why don't you tell them, Maurice? Tell them what you let them do to me." Machine stepped forward into the light, pulling off his jacket and tossing it aside. "Tell them how you sold us all out to that butcher Gadeaux."

"What's he talking about?" Cage shouted.

"You know, all this time, I couldn't figure out who had betrayed the team." Machine paced the floor. As he came closer, Phoe could see that the skin was gashed and peeling away. Pieces looked to be moldering and sloughing off with every movement. "I've been wracking my brain for years. After a while, I realized that it didn't matter. All of you betrayed me."

"You don't understand, Natalya…" Wilder pled. "I had no choice."

"There is always a choice," she screamed. "If nothing else, you could have killed me yourself. It would have been preferable to what Gadeaux did to me." She grinned, a horrible, wide maw that didn't look human. "But that's all right. Antonescu led me to him. And now there's only you, Maurice. And I will have my vengeance."

"Tell us," Cage coaxed. "Let us help you."

"I am beyond your help," she snarled, pulling at the skin on her face. The mask of Maurice fell away. The gray skin beneath was marked with deep scars. It looked as if her flesh had been eaten away by disease, but Phoe could see that she had once been a beautiful woman. Now there was nothing left. Only a mere hint of what she'd once been, now twisted and distorted by hate.

"I never meant for that to happen, Natalya," Maurice insisted. "I was trying to save our operation. The Quorti were relentless."

"What did you think would happen when you struck a bargain with vampires?" Natalya shouted. "You knew that the Quorti was looking for a way to create an army. You knew what they were up to, but you sold all of us out to save yourself."

"Then why did you kill the rest of them?" Cage asked. "They were your team. Your friends."

"They were puppets for MI Six just like you. They could have come back for me, but they scuttled away in the darkness like cockroaches. Cowards that were afraid of the Quorti."

Phoe heard the *sanguisuges* before she could see them. Their screams and groans echoed in the stairwell as they got closer. Out of the corner of her eye she could see them in the hall, fighting their way up the stairs, crawling over one another to get to them. There were men, women, and children, some of them still wearing the approved blazers with the Arrington crest on the pocket. It suddenly began to dawn on Phoe where the rest of the school was.

"Fuck," Phoe cursed. "Cage, we have to get Ben out of here." Cage tugged at the chains once more, but they weren't going anywhere.

"I can't free him," he said.

"Cage, look out," Phoe shouted, as the door burst open and the *sanguisuges* began to pour through the doors.

The first one landed on Cage's back, digging its claws into his shoulder. He shouted in pain, knocking it from his back. It tried to leap again, but Cage was fast, turning around and firing his autopistol into it twice through the head. Another was right behind it, then another, attacking him with a supernatural ferocity. They punched and scratched. Cage grabbed one by the throat, pulling it in and firing a bullet through the belly, then beating off the other with the writhing corpse.

"Phoe, get out of here," he shouted. "Take Ben and go."

"I won't leave you," she cried out, putting herself between Ben and the fight.

"Just do it."

She looked back at Ben then at Cage. Her only choice was to shift. She wasn't going to choose between the two people she loved most. Saying a silent prayer, she closed her eyes and willed the burning to begin.

With a scream, she was lifted off the floor. Her body contorted, taking on the shape of the bird. Long feathers grew from her back and arms, covering her. Her extremities began to burn, first in small flames and then bursting into an inferno that enveloped her entire body. Higher she rose until finally the transformation was complete and she heralded the rebirth of the phoenix with a cry that echoed through the room like a carillon.

"Phoe, no," Cage shouted.

But it was too late. She would have to deal with the consequences later, but Ben wasn't going to die if she could stop it. She darted around the room once, swooping down and grabbing some of the *sanguisuges* and throwing them against the wall, breaking them like statues. Then she swooped down to grab Ben in her talons. The boy whimpered, afraid of the creature. The chains were thick, but they were no match for the strength of the phoenix. They snapped, throwing sparks, and Ben screamed, but she was able to pull him free. With another shriek she darted out the broken window and flew him down to the safety of the garden between the wings of the building.

***

"Macijah."

Shots rang out across the room. Maurice was shooting wildly at the *sanguisuges* as they tried to get close. They exploded one by one. Their corpses were piling up and the others were grabbing them, desperate to drain whatever blood they had.

They hissed and growled at Cage, surrounding him. He bowed down, feeling the shift beginning. His body twisted and grew until he towered over them. His skin split at his spine, revealing a pelt of thick, silvery hair. His shout became a growl, then the roar of an enormous puma. The drones launched themselves at Cage, but they were no match for his size. He picked them off quickly, crushing several at once with each of his massive paws. One managed to get to his back, but Cage reached around with his neck and grabbed it with his teeth, crushing it instantly.

The smell of their blood was sour but inviting. His senses were enflamed with their scent and Cage could feel the rage taking over. His fangs grew, and his mouth watered. In a matter of minutes, most of the *sanguisuges* were gone, either dead or running blindly for their lives. He then turned on Maurice.

"Know that when he kills you, Maurice, I will take pleasure in taking your skin." Natalya grabbed him by the back of the neck, brandishing him at Cage and forcing him to his knees.

"I didn't make you what you are," Maurice shouted over the growling.

"Bullshit," Natalya shouted. "The Quorti bought and paid for you. The world will be a far better place when you're gone."

"Macijah, help me," Maurice shouted.

"You think he's going to help you? Why don't you tell him what really happened? Why don't you tell him that you ordered him dead? Tell him how you sent those beasts to kill him and his mate."

"Lies," Maurice whimpered. "She lies, Macijah. You and I are friends."

"You don't even know the meaning of the word," Natalya snarled.

"Macijah, you have to understand. I had to protect the organization. You have no idea the power that the Quorti has. I had no choice, Natalya." He dangled in her grasp. "They found us out. The Quorti was going to kill us if I didn't help them."

"And you would leave your friends to die to save your own skin. You coward." She threw Maurice at Cage's feet. "Feast on him. Take his blood. He betrayed us all."

Cage stared down at him, this pitiful, powerless man. All the rage he'd been harboring for years was bubbling there under the surface. A sniveling, conniving coward. His treachery had put them all in danger. If he let him live, the Quorti would continue to overrun the Earth, creating drones and slaves completely unchecked. But without Maurice, he'd never have found Phoe. Cage growled low, forcing Maurice to bow at his feet. He placed a paw against his back, holding him to the ground and looking up at Natalya.

"Sentimental fool. He deserves to die. As they all did." She pulled her gun, loaded with the slow-kill slugs and pointed it at Cage. "And if you're not with me, you're against me."

Before Natalya could pull the trigger, the call of the phoenix took her down. She covered her ears, dropping the gun and screaming with the piercing screech.

Phoe flew back in through the window and straight at Natalya's face. The woman tried to swat the bird away, but Phoe was nothing if not persistent. She dove, dragging the ends of her sharpened claws across Natalya's ruined cheek. With a call of triumph, Phoe swept downward and grabbed both Maurice and Natalya in her talons. They struggled in her grasp as she took them, rising high in the air and diving down across the courtyard to where a squad from B.E.A.S.T. waited.

Epilogue

Five Months Later

"I proudly present, Mr. and Mrs. Macijah St. John."

The crowd erupted in applause as Cage and Phoe appeared at the French doors leading out to the backyard tent where all their friends were waiting. Cage had been skeptical about having their wedding reception outside in April, but Phoe assured him that this was Louisiana. Spring in St. Francisville was like early summer most places. Besides, Miss Ava would have been heartbroken if they'd decided to have it anywhere else. It was her considered opinion that weddings were more special when you had them at home. That tended to be a southern eccentricity that even Phoe couldn't manage to understand. Two events that should happen at home were weddings and wakes.

Phoe and Cage waved to their guests and tried to walk down the steps to join them. Their photographer had different ideas and wanted them to stop and pose at every step. Finally, Cage walked up to the gentleman and took his camera. "Why don't you go take some pictures of the food, mate?"

She laughed, watching the man walk away. "Cage, that was rude."

"Sorry, but I've been standing in a church with that man taking photos of me from every angle. I'm sure he has at least twelve close-ups of my ass."

"Well I wouldn't hold that against him." She patted his tush then stretched up to kiss his cheek. "Besides, at least you aren't carrying thirty pounds of water and little girl on the front of your body."

"Oh my goodness," Miss Ava rushed toward them as they reached the tent, dragging Jessica behind her. "Where have you been? I told that photographer not to keep you too long. You shouldn't be on your feet."

"Miss Ava—" Phoe started.

"Oh, don't tell her anything, Miss Ava," Jess grumbled. "She knows *everything* about having babies."

Phoe rolled her eyes. She'd been arguing with these two for the last three months. When they first began planning the wedding, Phoe and Cage had set the date for the autumn. She hadn't wanted to get married looking like a knocked-up, white-trash princess. Jess was on her side until Miss Ava pointed out that their mother's heart would be broken if her little girl had a baby out of wedlock. So here she was, looking like a giant cupcake in miles of white organza.

"I'm fine," she stated firmly, not wanting to admit that her feet were killing her.

Jess and Miss Ava led Phoe down the hill to where everyone had gathered for the festivities. Her eyes glistened with tears as she saw how her friends had made such a beautiful reception. The tent was large and open with tiny white lights strung across the ceiling. A dance floor had been laid on one side with a bandstand where a live band played. Garlands made of pink and lavender spring flowers adorned everything. The round tables that had been scattered around offered a soft glow of illumination from the hurricane lamps in the middle of the centerpieces.

"Everything is so beautiful," she breathed, her voice cracking. "You guys really outdid yourselves."

"Well, Miss Ava did most of it," Jess said.

"Honey, it's been the thrill of my life to plan a wedding for you." The old woman hugged Phoe tightly. "I promised your Mama I'd take care of you, and I mean to do it."

"And since you and Cage will be spending more time here, it's only fitting that the whole town get involved. Ava and I did the flowers, but the catering was all Dr. Mariette. Then Flora and Gracie were here until midnight last night hanging those lights. Everyone is so happy for you."

"This could be the hormones talking, but... wow." Phoe embraced her sister and she couldn't help the tears. She'd never felt closer to Jess. She'd always wanted a sister that she could be friends with, but Jess always seemed so different. But Phoe realized in the last few years that nothing was more important than family. "I love you so much, sis. Thank you."

"Wow," Jess said. "No scolding about having sex with Stefan in the pantry just before the nuptials?"

"What?" Phoe asked, jerking away.

"Nothing," Jess replied. She shrugged and hugged Phoe again. "I love you too."

Whoever said that wedding receptions were for the bride and groom had obviously never been to one. The night progressed through dinner, a million toasts to the happy couple, and now the obligatory dancing, but still Phoe felt like she hadn't seen Cage since they had their kiss at the altar. She glanced across the room where Cage was currently dancing with Phoe's Aunt Lena. He was trying to smile, but Phoe could tell he was miserable. Not to mention that that poor half-dead dog was resting in the crook of his other arm.

"May I have a dance?"

Phoe turned and was surprised to find Vlad standing there. "Oh, wow, Vlad. I didn't think you'd come."

He shrugged. "Cage is a good friend. And his reception was at night, so how could I say no?" Phoe smirked and took his hand, allowing him to lead her out on to the dance floor. "Besides, I didn't want to miss my chance to have one dance with the bride." He twirled her around and pulled her back into his arms. "You look quite beautiful, Mrs. St. John."

"Thank you, Mr. Antonescu. Please try not to eat any of the guests."

"I'll try."

"I mean, it's a small town. There'd be talk."

Vlad laughed. "I've known Cage a long time, but I was pretty surprised when I found out he was retiring from BEAST to come and live here in Dogpatch."

"I beg your pardon. We're right outside of New Orleans. Hardly down in the holler," she drawled, putting it on thick. "At any rate, it wasn't much of a decision. The BEAST project is pretty much dead anyway with Maurice serving time on Kobi Six."

"It was. Until I agreed to take the director job."

Phoe gasped. "What? You? Really?"

"You say that like you don't think I can do it."

"Oh, no, no. Of course, you can do it. I wouldn't have imagined that you would want to."

Vlad shrugged. "I admit I had my reservations at first. After all, two of the best agents have decided to retire and have lots of babies. I can't promise I won't try to lure you back."

"Not a chance," Phoe stated. "As soon as Ben's adoption goes through, we're moving back here permanently."

"Do you really think you can escape this life? That you'll be satisfied with the real world?"

Phoe giggled. "The world is only as real as you make it, Vlad."

"There you are." Ben feigned annoyance as he stomped over to them, dragging Cage by the hand. "We been looking all over for you." He stepped in front of Vlad and sort of pushed him out of the way. The vampire winked at Phoe and clapped Cage on the shoulder.

"I'll be in touch." Vlad wandered away. Within seconds he'd caught the eye of one of Phoe's girlfriends and swept her onto the floor.

"What was that all about?" Cage asked.

"Nothing at all," Phoe answered with a grin.

Ben grabbed Phoe's hand and put it in Cage's. "It's time for you to dance."

"Oh really?" Cage asked. "Who died and made you dance boss?" Ben shrugged and walked off, leaving them on the dance floor.

The lights lowered, and the band began to play a slow song, one of Phoe's favorites. "Care to dance, Mrs. St. John?" Cage asked, offering his arm.

"I thought you'd never ask."

He led her onto the dance floor and everyone moved aside. Her heart fluttered as he pulled her close. Coordination had never been her strong suit and now everyone was watching.

"Feeling all right?" he asked.

"A little tired. But otherwise okay. You?"

"I'm good. Ollie said I should have another drink to loosen me up."

She laughed. "Do you need loosening up?"

"I didn't think so. Ollie was pretty loose though." He gestured over to where Ollie was sitting by the bar chatting up the bartender.

"He must still be licking his wounds over my sister."

"Maybe a little. I told him not to worry too much. Stef's pretty fickle. Jess may need a shoulder to cry on soon."

Phoe nestled in against him, closing her eyes and letting Cage lead her, drawing on his strength. "You know, I've been doing a lot of thinking the last couple of days."

"Always dangerous."

"You've taught me so much. I used to be scared of my own shadow, but you taught me to be strong. To stand up for myself and those who can't stand up for themselves. I never thanked you for that."

"You never have to."

"And I was thinking that, you know, if you didn't want to retire. I mean, I'd…" Her words trailed off as a sudden, sharp wave of pain hit and she gasped. "Oooh… damn."

"What?"

"Ow. A little bit of pain there." She stopped and leaned against Cage for a moment, waiting for it to subside.

"What kind of little pain?"

"The kind that hurts," she seethed as another pang hit. "I, uh, I think I need to sit down for a second."

Cage put his arm around her waist and walked her toward their table across the tent. "Is this like the little pain before?"

"Uhm, I'm not sure." Phoe sighed. "Feel free to ask it. Owie."

Miss Ava must have seen the look on Phoe's face because she rushed over and took her other arm. "Are you all right?"

"I'm not sure," she replied, looking up at Cage. "But, I think I might be having some contractions."

Miss Ava let out a shriek that made Aunt Lena's dog howl. "Jessica. Oliver. Get over here. Phoebe's in labor."

Suddenly, the entire reception was in chaos. Phoe could feel herself turning bright red as seemingly the whole town rushed over to see if they could help. All of them offering words of wisdom.

"It's okay, Phoebe, darlin'. Women have babies every day."

"You know, back in the Bible times people would just squat in the dirt, pop out the kid, and go back to their fields."

"Make sure you do that Maze breathin'."

"I knew a lady who broke her water at the Piggly Wiggly…"

The next thing she knew Cage and Vlad were walking her to the car while Jessica waved them toward the vehicle like Phoebe was a plane shuttling out to the runway. They piled her into the car and she pulled Cage into the back seat with her.

"Vlad, get us to the hospital. And try not to hit anything."

"I'll try, but your cars in this country… the steering wheel is on the wrong side."

He pulled out of the driveway of the house, taking out one of the signs that said "Congratulations Cage and Phoe" and kicking up dust all over their guests as they tore out of the yard and into the street. Everything was happening so fast. And despite all their previous adventures, Phoe was terrified.

But as she looked up into Cage's face, she realized she didn't ever have to be afraid again. Of anything.

Because he would always be there.

Now and forever.

Phoe and Cage thank you for standing by their side through all their adventures. Actually, Cage thinks the lot of you are bloody wankers for minding his business, but he knows Phoe appreciates it, and he'll do anything to make her happy… so thanks.

ABOUT THE AUTHOR

Alexandra Christian is an author of mostly romance with a speculative slant. She's committed to bringing exciting stories and sapiosexual love monkeys to intelligent readers everywhere. Lexx also likes to keep her fingers in lots of different pies having written everything from sci-fi and horror to Sherlock Holmes adventures as her alter ego, A.C. Thompson.

A self-proclaimed "Southern Belle from Hell," Lexx is a native South Carolinian who lives with an epileptic wiener dog and her husband, author and ghost hunter, Tally Johnson. Her long-term aspirations are to one day be a best-selling authoress and part-time pinup girl. She's a member of Romance Writers of America. Questions, comments and complaints are most welcome at her website: http://lexxxchristian.wixsite.com/alexandrachristian.

ALSO BY ALEXANDRA CHRISTIAN

Naked
NeoGeisha
In Absinthia

www.BOROUGHSPUBLISHINGGROUP.COM

If you enjoyed this book, please write a review. Our authors appreciate the feedback, and it helps future readers find books they love. We welcome your comments and invite you to send them to info@boroughspublishinggroup.com. Follow us on Facebook, Twitter and Instagram, and be sure to sign up for our newsletter for surprises and new releases from your favorite authors.

Are you an aspiring writer? Check out www.boroughspublishinggroup.com/submit and see if we can help you make your dreams come true.